Ever Darkening

Janeal Falor

To learn more about this author, please visit:
www.janealfalor.com

Cover by Alisha at Damonza

Other Books By Janeal Falor:
Mine to Tarnish (Mine #.5)
You Are Mine (Mine #1)
Mine to Spell (Mine #2)

To Erik
For loving me even when things are dark

Table of Contents

Chapter One

I'm the one chosen to save the entire world from evil. Even at the age of ten, I know enough for that to give me knots of tension.

"Are you still sure I'm the one?" I ask the Astra, our leader, as she prunes her struggling vine climbing the side of her cabin.

She stops her clipping to give me her full attention instead of just part of it, as she has the rest of my lesson on good and evil. "More certain than when you were called. You are meant to destroy the last of the evil in this world, Kaylyn."

I rub the hilt of my sword—a burden from the moment I received it. Someday, when I'm grown, it will be full size, and I will have to slice into men and women. Not as an evil murderer but as a bringer of good and peace. "It just seems like such a big task."

She places a hand on my shoulder, strong despite her many wrinkles. "It is, my child. But you have it within you to accomplish great things." She returns to cutting back the vine. "It's like this plant. It was growing before, but after I cut it back, it will thrive. It needs conflict. You are just like it. The harder things get for you, the greater you will become."

The last thing I want is to be cut down. But the Astra smiles so sweetly, and I have learned a lot in the last four years. Somehow I'll make it happen.

"Besides, we're giving you all the training and power we can to aid you." She cuts off another long vine. "Now run along and play. Stars know you don't have as much time for it as you should."

"Yes, Astra."

I hurry as fast as when I'm training, searching for Jorrin and Marsa, my two very best friends. It doesn't take long to find them in the forest on the mountain. Marsa is sitting on a log, giggling, while Jorrin looks like he's dancing around the grove of trees.

"You're just in time," Marsa says, her blonde hair twirling as she looks toward me. "Jorrin's going to catch a squirrel."

Thank the moon the Astra released me from lessons when she did! "What will you do after you catch it?"

"Let it go, of course," he replies, his smile wide.

"Perfect. Why haven't you caught one yet, then?"

Even though he's only a year older than me, he puffs out his chest like he's one of the grown Zophas warriors. He waits a moment, and we're all quiet until a squirrel comes near. It never takes long to find them in the forest that's

2

around our home.

I laugh as Jorrin dives for the squirrel and misses by inches. He grins at me as if the whole point of his actions is to get me to laugh. Something warms in me then. Something strong and unfamiliar and not entirely just friendship.

As he jumps to try and catch the squirrel again, Marsa leans over and whispers, "Someday, I'm going to marry him."

The new feeling within my heart clamps down with twisting pain that juts through me. It's fine if she marries him. The new feeling was just our growing friendship anyway. I used some of her mother's attention when she took me in. I can't take her future husband's attention as well.

"I'll help make it happen." My vow is even more solemn than when I promised to do my all as the one chosen to defeat evil.

"You're not just my best friend," Marsa says. "You're like my sister. The best sister ever."

I grin at her, the last of the pain that clamped around my heart releasing. We'll be together forever because of it.

Jorrin strolls out from a group of trees, gently petting a squirrel held close to him. "Guess they like it better when you ask nicely instead of jumping after them."

"You did it," I exclaim.

He gives a sheepish grin. "I did offer him some nuts."

"That just means you're smart," Marsa says.

As Jorrin comes closer, he holds the squirrel out to me. "Would you like to hold it?"

The clamping in my chest is back, fiercer than ever, but I temper it with the knowledge that I'm helping my best friend. She did call me her sister. Sisters we will be. "After Marsa."

"Really?" Marsa is already reaching to pet the squirrel. "He's such a cute little guy."

For a moment, Jorrin's expression darkens into something hidden and wholly unfamiliar. But then the expression is gone, quicker than it came. Everything is good. Or as good as it's supposed to be with evil still in the world. The Astra is right, however. I can do my job as the chosen one. I will defeat all evil and leave the world a perfectly good place for everyone, including Marsa and Jorrin. I will fulfill my duty as the chosen one.

Chapter Two

Seven Years Later

Being the one chosen to kill the entire evil population is a burden heavier than sin. Not that I know what it's like to sin, but I imagine this is worse. Killing is never taken lightly, even when sanctioned by our leaders, the same leaders who chose me to carry it out. I've lost count of how many Malryx I've executed for that exact reason. And now there is only one left. Only one evil being. My purpose of being is almost complete.

As I sit alone on the mountain, daylight filtering through the trees, I'm not quite sure what to think about my task almost being accomplished. It's one thing to know Malryx murder, kidnap, steal, and do numerous other things, and even to see them do so in person. But to be the one in charge of eliminating such people? It's a lot to take in.

They've been around as long as anyone can remember, until I finish them off. Even after all these years, the talk I had with the Astra still comes to me in perfect detail. Our talk doesn't seem to make the pressure any easier to handle, no matter how hard I think on it.

I've spent enough time wondering about it, though. It's time to head back to the others and find out if there is any news on where the last Malryx is so I can track him down. He's been cunning, giving us trouble finding him. Hopefully, that will end soon.

I head toward the top of the mountain, wondering who will be there and what news they'll have. I flex my power out as I go—a habit no longer needed since only one Malryx is left, and he wouldn't dare show himself around so many of us. It would mean certain death for him. Still, I stretch out my Zophasken. Looking for danger has become such a habit, I can't help it.

It flows over the land, finding nothing but the plants and animals as usual, but at the top of the mountain where I'm headed are a good dozen sparks of light. The spots of goodness against my own power are soothing. I focus on them as I move closer, but as my power expands outward, something isn't right. There's a flicker of darkness. Of evil.

How can that be? I thought no one knew where he was. Something must have happened in the few hours I took for myself—at Showna's command. The leader of our band of fighters was insistent I needed the time. Now I'm not so sure it was the thing needed most. I move faster, legs straining, familiar as the hurried pace may be.

Darkness draws nearer to the mountaintop, slinking closer to home where there's only light while I approach. Fallen branches crack beneath my feet as I race there. Maybe someone is bringing the last Malryx. The last evil man. Morphrac. But the thought is in vain even before I think it. The darkness is alone, trailing continually nearer. No light accompanies it. Everyone is gathering just outside the cave in a bright burst of light. They must know. They must feel it coming.

Then why aren't they doing anything?

They must be waiting for me.

But why is he coming to us after hiding for so long?

The sound of my boots grows faint as I reach our clearing. From the amount of blood soaking Showna's tunic and pooling on the ground, she has little time left, no matter what I do. The sight stops me, and I almost fall to the stones beneath me. I tilt forward but don't let myself go. Those gathered around her part, making a place for me, but they don't leave her side.

They aren't waiting for me. The bright spots are waiting for our leader, Showna, to die. My adoptive mother.

Knowing it's too late, that it won't do any good, I kneel down and reach out to examine her injuries.

"Leave it," Showna croaks out.

I grab her hand instead of checking her

wounds. Next to me, her daughter, Marsa, calls out, "Momma, no." Marsa sobs. "She can fix you."

"It's my time." Showna gasps for breath and looks straight at me. "And yours."

"Momma." Marsa's big eyes are filled with tears, and her usually laughing mouth is cinched with pain.

My own pulse quickens, energy infusing me. And guilt. Even if the moment I've trained for my whole life has come, it's wrong to be this eager for it as Showna lies dying. If I had been with her, if she hadn't sent me away, if my moment had come sooner, she wouldn't be leaving. "Don't talk anymore. Save your strength. I'll find him."

"Good. I know your final battle will be won." Her breathing is wet.

I don't know which is worse, her dying or her words. That Morphrac, the last evil, the darkness coming to my home, killed her because of me.

The others shift beside us, but I don't let them distract me. I don't let the pain and sadness scratching at me inside. Now is not the time for distractions.

"Those of you—" Showna coughs, a hacking, pitiful sound. Someone offers a water skin, but she waves it away. "If you haven't... given Kaylyn your power..."

"Hush now," I say. "I'll be fine. I'll defeat Morphrac for you as I am. The Aster and Astra said I can do this."

She doesn't seem to hear me. At this point, I can't tell if it's intentional or delirium from blood loss. "Give Zophasken... to Kaylyn. She's our best cha..." She draws out the word but never gets to finish it.

My throat tightens as her life withdraws. I won't cry. Not now.

Marsa pulls Showna to her, heedless of the blood soaking her clothes. "No, Momma! Don't leave me!"

What does one do in this situation? I've seen much death but never my best friend's mother. The woman who is in almost every respect my own mother. And evil is still coming. I can feel the darkness closing in on us. There's not much time before it's here.

"Showna was right," Jorrin says, his tall height empowering his words. "Kaylyn is our best chance."

I meet his eyes, the coolness of the stone floor finally registering. He reaches down for me, his grip firm and warm as he helps me up. Once I'm standing, he doesn't let go. Instead, he closes his other hand around mine, tender and comforting. With something else hovering just on the edge.

I'm grateful I've done this before so it's a familiar process, though it doesn't get any easier with repetition.

"My Zophasken is yours." Jorrin's deep voice thrums through me.

His power washes over me, his goodness flowing to me in vast waves. He's strong. So much stronger than me. Why did the Aster and Astra not choose him for this? Not only is he one of our best fighters, but he's also unfailingly good. Only last week, he stayed to practice with me when all the others had long since gone to bed. When we finished, he pulled out some food he'd set aside from dinner, knowing I hadn't stopped practicing long enough to eat. And it's not just his power that is strong but him as well. He's tough from years of fighting.

No wonder Marsa is in love with him.

When his Zophasken grows low, I stop the flow. Still plenty of good left within him. The memory of having to defeat another Malryx after taking too much is still a powerful reminder. It's not a mistake I'll ever make again.

He gives my hand a quick squeeze before moving away. His power hums within me, sunny and comforting, as it merges with mine. The others take turns coming to me as quickly as they can, relinquishing their powers to me so rapidly, it's hard to keep track of them all. It only takes a moment to get through the last of those who haven't already gifted their Zophasken.

Not one of them hesitates to share what they know I'll need. Perhaps if Showna would have also shared their powers, she'd still be with us. But the Aster and Astra insisted I am the one extra Zophasken should be given to. I am the one to finish the quest that began hundreds of years ago.

I am the one to defeat the last evil person alive.

I just don't know why.

By the time Azleco, another Zophas, steps to me, I'm tingling with an overabundance of power. I'm not used to getting so much at once. I've been getting it from just a person or two at a time for years. With Marsa's grief, I didn't expect her to even notice us. But when Azleco finishes, Marsa is waiting her turn. Though her eyes are red-rimmed, they're dry. She takes my hand with hers, one of the few places not marred by her mother's blood.

"I can do this," I say.

"I know." Her voice cracks with grief held at bay. "My Zophasken is yours."

And it is. Her strength rushes into me, merging with my own and all that many others have given me. Its warmth is a balm against the ache from Showna's death, which I've been trying to ignore. I let the power soothe me as it slides into place. When I've taken some but left enough for her to stay strong, I don't let go. Instead, I embrace her, not caring about Showna's blood getting on me.

"I can't lose you too," she whispers, voice desperate.

I keep my words faint, for her ears alone as I hug her. "Nothing will happen to me, and your mother's death won't be in vain. I'll defeat Morphrac. The planet will be rid of Malryx. Your mother's dream to get rid of all evil will come true."

She sniffs and starts crying again. I motion for someone to take my place, hoping Jorrin will, but Tavo moves forward before Jorrin has a chance. As long as someone is here to help, it will be enough. There will be time for her and me to comfort each other later. After I kill Morphrac.

I pull away, and Tavo puts an arm around her. She'll be fine.

Something breaks close by with a loud crash.

Morphrac.

"Come out to play, my little Zophaslings," he calls from a distance, though too close to our sanctuary for comfort. "Or did slaughtering your leader leave you too scared to face me?"

I don't let anger rise within me, though it wants to. Instead, I channel everything I've been taught for the last seventeen years into what's to come. It's not for revenge over Showna that I'm doing this. It's for the calling I've been given. It's for her dream and the dream of those before her.

Everyone stares at me. Not frowning but not smiling either. What's the appropriate expression for this moment? With Showna's death and our possible victory so close together, I'm not sure. I draw my sword and settle on giving them my most determined look.

"Let us come with you and help," Jorrin says.

Without their power, they're more likely to be a hindrance than a help. "Thank you, but I will do this," I say. "Stay in the cave until I get back."

"Vitliruc," Jorrin says.

"Vitliruc, my friend," Marsa says.

"Vitliruc." The others join in.

I nod in acknowledgment of their good wishes and then leave as they carry Showna's body into the cave.

No Morphrac in sight. I stretch my Zophasken, readying it to feel the burn of his darkness as I move away from the cave. My power flows through me, dancing through every corner of my being. I stretch it away from me and to the mountain I'm on. It flows from me smoother and easier than ever, strong in its grandeur.

There's no Malryx in the immediate area. Did he give his taunt and then run like a coward?

Something's wrong.

As I walk away from my home, I push my power out farther, searching the area for his stain. Nothing. He's backtracked more than when I first arrived. Why is he so anxious to get away after invading our territory in the first place? I shove my Zophasken, rippling it from me down the slope, but there's still no sign of

13

his taint. Just the soothing hum of nature's neutrality.

Overhead, the sky is a perfect blue, light and clear. A few puffs of pristine clouds power across it. But far off in the distance, past the village, forests, plains, and mountains shorter than my own, the blue gives way to a faint hint of darkened sky.

Will the heavens rain down on us tonight? This, our night of mourning? And our night of celebration after I kill Morphrac? Tears for all those we've lost in the journey and a fresh new beginning. Fitting and possible... if I can find Morphrac before the clouds get here.

Yet, there's nothing. The surrounding area is empty. For all his taunts and reputation, Morphrac appears to be a wimp. No doubt he's waiting somewhere with poison darts. Or perhaps he'll try to shoot me with an arrow from behind. I've lost to both of these tricks before, but I won't stoop to the same level.

Instead, I let more of my Zophasken slide from me and pour into the cracks and shadows that evil may hide in. It billows from me, searching far past where I'm used to. Its strength tries to let loose from me, but I keep a tight grip on it lest it be uncontrolled and useless. Soon, it'll be a natural extension of me.

I study where my power touches and try to decide where to search next. The world is laid out before me as I stand on the mountain's peak. Air swirls around me, warmed by a false return to summer. Through the forest on the mountainside, I can see a little of the closest village far below in the valley. A stream from a nearby river flows through it. There's a clearing, then an expanse of forest on the other side. My Zophasken moves through it all. No slithering darkness. Where could he be?

I scan the forest with both my vision and my Zophasken one last time. I can't see far, but my power feels the lack of human life. I turn toward the other side of the mountain, my power moving across the world as I do so. A heavy, dark splotch mars the world.

There's a reason he won't attack me. A whole group of them.

Fool.

I whirl toward the cave where I left the others.

The trees blur as I rush by. My power snaps back in my haste, but it doesn't matter now. I know where he's going. He's not there yet but will be before I can make it. I hope their combined skills are enough to fight him off until I reach them. With so little power left, they won't know he's coming. Why did I leave them?

Marsa. Jorrin. Tavo. Felix. Sosha. Azleco.

Am I to have their deaths on me, too?

They gave me their power, and I sped off without a thought. My legs and lungs burn, but I press on. I've been doing this long enough; I should have known he'd go after them. I was too caught up in my own triumph. It will be a hollow victory should he kill them before I've dealt his punishment. The cave and Morphrac are nearing. Almost there.

My foot catches on a rock. The ground rushes toward me. I twist, landing on my side instead of my face. Pain jars through my arm. Not broken or seriously injured. I ignore it and jump back to my feet, but evil looms close, chuckling.

I spin to face Morphrac, trying not to let my relief that he didn't make it to the others show. His looks don't even hint at the darkness that lies within him, scorching my Zophasken. He's deceptively handsome, like many Malryx are. Dark hair, dark eyes. Shorter than me but muscular. A face that says, "marry me," not "all the evil left in the world is in me."

"Your last apprentice was bigger," I say, hoping to buy time to catch my breath.

"He could have handled you." His voice is smooth and rich.

"He didn't."

Morphrac spits. "You lie."

"You know Zophas never lie."

His lips thin and eyes narrow at the truth he doesn't want to admit. Malryx never see me for the threat I am.

"You had help," he says.

"Not for him. I dealt his punishment alone. Gelpeta, though—Showna and I took him down together." I bend my knees. "And now it's your

16

turn."

"You don't know what you're getting into, girl."

"I'm ridding this world of the last scum. Peace will finally be ours."

He grins. Not the response I usually get.

I blast him with my power, a bursting, white-hot fireball charged with good against his evil. Zophasken against his Malkine power. Then I rush at him. Our swords clang as they meet. The sound rings through the air, invigorating me, but his jabs are already slacking. Was he the leader of the Malryx only for his planning? It can't have been for his fighting skills.

The brightness of my Zophasken is tainted as his Malkine arcs toward me. No way I'm letting his power weaken my own. I push back, my light easily overcoming his darkness. His sword falls to the ground. It hasn't even been a full minute since our blades met.

All the years I trained. The power I was given. It must have paid off. Killing Morphrac, the last of the evil, is the easiest punishment I've administered. But killing is still hard, even if it's for good. Taking a life is something the Malryx do. Except in situations as this where the Aster and Astra have passed judgment. Morphrac is responsible for the torture and death of countless innocents. If allowed to live, no doubt he'd be responsible for countless more—and who knows what other catastrophes.

I press my sword against his neck. "Are you willing to change your ways?"

He laughs.

No, then. Not unexpected, but a girl can hope.

Chapter Three

Jorrin wraps the cut on my arm. Though strong from years of fighting, his fingers are gentle. My arm may be thin, but it's all muscle, and the blade didn't go too deep. The wound will heal long before my emotions.

"The ceremony is starting soon," Marsa says from behind Jorrin, pulling me back to what is about to take place. Of what never should have happened.

None of us move. My body is sore from the fight, but it's nothing I'm not used to. Really, it's not even bad. I'm just not sure I know how to handle what's to come. It's so much easier to deal with what I know. To worry about defending the people.

"I thought it would be harder to defeat Morphrac," I say.

"Give yourself some credit," Marsa says. "You've always been the best of us. That's why you were chosen. The Aster and Astra knew you would be able to do it."

Which is why Showna would still be alive if I'd been with her. Though as easy as he was to beat, I'm surprised Morphrac killed her. She should have at the very least been able to hold him off until I got there. "Maybe, but I guess I expected something more. I've fought tougher opponents."

"He was their leader," Jorrin says. "Maybe he only excelled at leading and not actual fighting?" But from the look in his eye, I can tell he's not sure he believes the idea either. And it doesn't explain how Morphrac killed Showna. The two ideas don't go together. Though maybe there was more to their fight than I know. With both of them dead, we'll never understand.

"We're going to be late if we don't leave now," Marsa says.

That's finally enough to get us moving. Not that they'd start without us, but one shouldn't be late. Jorrin stands and grabs my hand to help me do the same. Of course I don't need help standing. And as much as I appreciate the thought, having such contact seems wrong in front of Marsa. I quickly drop his hand and head down the mountain, hurrying to put distance between us. Between what should and shouldn't be.

Still, as we walk it's hard not to think of the two behind me, walking side by side. Jorrin with his deep brown hair, hazel eyes, and strong build next to Marsa's light frame, big blue eyes, and blonde hair. They look good together. They make the perfect couple.

When we arrive at the village, Showna's remains are already waiting on the unlit pyre, where we will release her soul to the stars so she can watch over us. There's a pang in my chest. I don't know if I want to get closer to say a proper goodbye or back away. I do know this is wrong—all wrong. She was strong. The one who worked so hard to make my destiny come to pass. Our leader. Our hope.

Jorrin stops by me, Marsa on his other side. Maybe now she'll finally be able to feel the love that she wants. The love from him she's been waiting for. What a morbid time to think such things, but it's what Showna would have wanted.

It looks as if the whole village has gathered around the pyre. So many cared about Showna. Even some I don't recognize. Word must have spread fast if those from other villages had time to get here. If they waited to do the ceremony, I'm sure the whole valley would be brimming with people to see her to the sky. Those who are here are many, but they are silent, even the young ones, as they wait and watch.

We hover at the back of the group, though most of them turn to look at us as we join. Or maybe they aren't looking at us. Maybe just at me. I'm used to being watched often, taken in as I help rid different villages of the evil that plagues them. But it's always easier when someone else is with me. When others help to take the watchful eyes from just me. I ignore the gazes the best I can. We're here to remember Showna, and that's what I'm going to do.

I let my arms hang loose at my side. The

Astra and Aster are together in front of the pyre, their black ceremonial robes flowing to the ground, dotted with silver like the night sky. Both of them have long hair and crinkled faces. I remember them looking like this even when I was young and they first worked with me. They will one day grow old and die, and a new Aster and Astra will take their places, but it's hard to think of that ever coming to pass. They are dear friends and trusted counselors, even if I don't always like what they have to say.

"Showna was an incomparable leader and friend," the Astra begins. Even from back here, I can see her hazel eyes are bright with unshed tears.

Her words continue, but it's hard to focus on them. They mush like too many opponents in a fight, clashing and clanking together. Marsa sniffs. I reach across Jorrin and hand her my handkerchief. It's new. I haven't used it to clean my sword yet, so for once I don't have to worry over loaning it out. I suppose I won't need to use it anymore. There's nothing left to use my sword for. My handkerchiefs will have to be for things girls normally use them for, like blotting noses and waving at boys. The thought makes the pang in my chest grow. I grip the hilt of my sword and clench my fingers around it until they ache.

Jorrin wraps an arm around Marsa, who struggles not to openly weep, her eyes blinking furiously as she pants those hitching breaths she did when her pet rabbit died. She leans into Jorrin, his presence no doubt easing the pain or at least helping to soothe it. Yes. Soon her wish of getting the attention from him she's always wanted will be granted. The sight makes me uncomfortable, probably because I'm not used to seeing more than sibling-like affection.

I focus on the Aster, who is now speaking. His deep voice is soothing, but it's still difficult for me to concentrate enough for the words to make sense. I give up trying and instead look at the pyre, carefully stacked up and adorned with flowers. A pyre fit for the best.

Showna. I miss her already. The only woman I remember as my mother, who took me in when my own parents died in a Malryx attack. She could have given me to another family, one with both the husband and wife still alive, unable to have children and aching for their own. But she kept me. She must have seen something in me, even back when I was a little one. She raised me. Taught me. Trained me. Loved me. Marsa became my sister. Showna, my mother. And I returned her kindness by leaving her alone to fight Morphrac.

The wind picks up, swirling a cold breeze as the Aster falls silent. Just as well since I wasn't listening. He may have grown up with Showna, but he couldn't have known her like we did. The breeze settles down, but the chill remains.

A villager hands the Aster a torch, and with

it, he glides forward. Head bowed, he places the torch against a piece of wood until it lights. The crackle quickly fills the air. After a minute of silence, the Aster says, "If any would like to speak of Showna, please take this opportunity to do so."

No one steps forward. Instead, everyone's gazes turn toward me. And they should. With her dead, I'm the next in line to lead. I have the confidence of the Aster and Astra behind me. I have the greatest Zophasken within me, its power almost consuming whenever I think on it. By all rights, I am the Zophas' leader now.

But I'm not. Not really.

There's nothing left to fight. There's no reason for us to even have a leader against evil. We'll rely wholly on the Aster and Astra now. We Zophas won't be needed any longer. Those of us who haven't already will become a helpful part of society another way. No more need for warriors. No more need for fighting. No more need for everything I was trained for. Especially this. I was trained to fight, not talk.

After several moments of silence, Marsa, stars sing her praise, steps forward and speaks, her voice surprisingly clear considering the tears on her cheeks.

"Mother was unlike the rest of us. She helped pave the way for us to have freedom from the Malryx. More than anyone else, she would have realized what has been accomplished this day and want it celebrated. I only wish she'd lived a little longer to see it."

She steps back next to Jorrin and lifts her face to the sky. *The clouds I saw in the distance didn't move fast enough to make it here tonight. Perhaps tomorrow they will come, but for now, Showna's path to the heavens is clear.*

Others speak. Some say few words; some say many. All mourn Showna. Most also acknowledge her dream come to pass. Our victory and freedom. The fire is smoldering when no one else speaks. The Aster and Astra move closer to the coals. They reach into their pouches and throw something onto the embers. Flames flash from them.

"We release you to the stars," they say together.

And there's nothing left to hold her spirit here. She's free from this life. Free to watch from above, where the stars give direction. Not free to be with us, though. I press my teeth together to keep my jaw from trembling.

"Please, go and enjoy the festivities," the Aster says. "We have the peace Showna and many others always dreamed from the evil people of this world. Let us celebrate that."

It doesn't take much prompting. Though the people loved Showna, this moment has been coming for many lifetimes. *It's just as well. It's true Showna would rather us be celebrating than mourning. That doesn't make moving from my spot any easier. The other Zophas, both current and ones who have moved on, must feel the* same way. The villagers leave with a nod or a hug, as if they know we need the time.

No matter that there's much to celebrate and that it's what Showna would have wanted. There's still a throb in my chest at seeing how quickly they leave.

Once everyone else is gone, the Zophas all look to me, but I still have nothing to say. I stop myself from rubbing my toe against the ground. Now is not the time to be weak. They need strength. I look to the heavens, wishing Showna would send some sort of sign or direction. I see nothing but thousands of twinkling stars, warmed by all the souls of the good who have passed on.

I look at those still gathered. They have followed my example and are staring at the stars. This is the best I can give them, to honor those who have gone before us. Slowly, they look at me again, one by one. When everyone's attention is back on me, I simply nod.

We've worked and trained together enough that they know and understand me almost as well as Marsa and Jorrin do. They follow after the crowd in twos and threes, heading for the celebration. Though maybe with not so light of step as the others.

Jorrin moves toward the Zophas, giving Marsa and me a backward glance. He stops close to the cooling coals. Far enough to give us space but close enough to be supportive.

Marsa holds out my handkerchief. "Thank

you."

"Keep it." After today, I've no further use for it.

"Just as well. My tears and snot are all over it."

We chuckle together but not in our usual, full way. We're both too somber to be any good at laughing.

She glances at Jorrin. I follow her gaze and say quietly, "Have you said anything to him yet?"

"No, but I'm certain he's guessed my feelings by now."

"Then perhaps you should get him to the festival, where you can cheer each other up. Showna would have been delighted to welcome a son-in-law to celebrate evil being eliminated."

Marsa blushes. "A proposal is unlikely tonight, let alone a wedding."

"You've waited long enough." Indeed, we both have. Most girls get married by sixteen, if they hold off that long. Even a year past that feels like too much for the villagers to understand. "At least tonight can get you started in the right direction."

Saying all this is right for her, but it pricks at me. Marsa must detect that. Of course she does. She wraps me in a hug. "Don't fret, sister. We will find you a match soon enough."

Soon enough for what? I look at Jorrin, who is patiently waiting, and reluctantly release her. "Go on. I'll be along shortly."

"Don't be too long. It's past time you learn to dance and play." She heads for Jorrin.

He turns at the sound of her boots crunching toward him, her skirt swaying. Maybe I should have changed into something nicer, too, but I'm still in my usual attire. Dark brown breeches and shirt. The better to blend into nature with.

Jorrin smiles at her, but when she tries to lead him away, he looks back at me, feet unmoving. Marsa says something to him, and I give a little wave toward the party. He turns his gaze from me, although slower than I expected, and together they leave, but he keeps glancing backward.

The party is close but far enough that it's not easy to see in the dark. A large fire brightens the right; torches leave specks of light all around the side. Shadows and light are all I can make out from here, though the sound travels easily. Shouts of joy and laughter. Music bouncing through the night air.

The revelries make me long to train with my sword. Without moving from my place, I squat, not letting the ground dirty my pants. I wrap my arms around my bent legs, rest my head on my knees, and stare at the faint glow of coals.

I've never attended a celebration before. All the times I was invited, I had to leave beforehand to carry out a request from the Aster or Astra. Or I would be making plans, tracking down Malryx. It's one of the few places I belong during such parties. Where I used to belong. Celebrating like the others—not so much. With the others is where I should be now, though. Dancing and feasting and doing whatever it is they do to revel in the good things of life.

I meditate for a few minutes, clearing my mind of everything. But I can't stay like this forever. The others will worry if I don't make an appearance. I can't keep putting it off. I must go. Standing, I reach my hands high above me and stretch out my body while ignoring the pain in my arm. The kinks don't ease like usual.

I take one last look at the night sky. The stars Showna has joined glitter. What's it like up there? What does she think of it? Is she happy to know we've succeeded? Glad to see us celebrating? Or does she even notice or care now?

With a sigh, I tread toward the celebration.

ॐ∾

The festivities are roaring. Drums are being tapped. Stringed instruments are being plucked. Feet are stomping and hands clapping. Couples dance in the clearing. Spinning, twisting, laughing. Tables are filled with food, more than I've ever seen at one time before. Unfortunately, I'm not even hungry. But others are. They cluster around the tables, eating and talking.

Everyone seems to be smiling. It's all so loud and fast and bright.

Jorrin and Marsa are by one of those tables, but before I can go to them, a new song starts. Marsa says something to him, and Jorrin leads her to the clearing. I hang back in the fringes, watching them dance. He twirls her and throws her in the air with strength fitting a Zophas. Others around them do variations of the same thing. It's like random chaos. I've never seen anything like it.

The music is loud—almost too loud, but it makes me feel like moving. Maybe I should get the musicians to play their songs while I train. Though I guess it's something I should have done a long time ago. It's hard to remember I don't need to train anymore.

My throat tightens. This was a bad idea. I turn to hike up the mountain toward my room. Or at least some place empty and quiet. A boy of about thirteen stops in front of me. Stick arms and legs. Unruly orange hair falling in his eyes. No threat.

I'm about to brush past him when he says, "You're her, aren't you? Kaylyn?"

I stare him down, not sure I like hearing my name with this sort of awe. "I am."

His grin widens. "Thank you! Thank you! I want to be a Zophas like you when I grow up."

Before I can think of a reply, he hustles over to a group of boys. His friends, I assume by the way they punch him on the shoulder and pat his back. They gesture at me. Tentatively, I raise my hand in the air and give it a twitch. Every one of them waves back, their chatter growing along with their praise toward the orange-haired boy. It's almost like congratulations after beating a Malryx. Of course, no matter what he wants, he can't be a Zophas. The thought makes me cringe.

I glance over my shoulder at the dancing. Marsa and Jorrin are still twirling and laughing. My chest twists as they smile at each other. Though they trained with me all while growing up, the last couple of years there have been fewer Malryx to hunt after, so they've been spending more time with the villagers. The only reason I didn't join is because the Aster and Astra said they saw something more in me. Something they thought we would need.

They must have been right. I did defeat many Malryx, including Morphrac. Rid the world of evil. Yet I can't help wondering, if they had chosen someone else, would that person have met my same success? If someone else had gotten the extra training and Zophasken I received, instead of me, couldn't they have done what I did? Sometimes it was hard. Beyond difficult, in fact. Too many times I thought I wouldn't succeed. And defeating Morphrac? That was easy. Almost too easy.

The song ends, the cheering afterward disrupting my thoughts. Jorrin catches my eye and pulls Marsa toward me, laughing their way over. No escaping the festivities now.

"Thank you," Marsa says to Jorrin as they reach me. Her face glows with more than just the torchlight.

"My pleasure." He turns to me. "What about you, Kaylyn? Would you like to dance?"

Something almost familiar, like a faint memory, races through me at the thought. It's not entirely unpleasant but not comfortable either. I eye those gathering for the next song. Boys on one side of the clearing, girls lined up on the other. I'd rather hunt down another Malryx than join them. Except I can't do that anymore. What am I to do now?

I say, "I don't know how to dance."

"I can teach you. It's easy."

"He really is great," Marsa adds. "I'm sure he can help."

The drums beat, and soon the lively fiddles join them. The boys and girls meet in the middle and twirl around each other. They briefly touch hands, then back away from each other before doing it again. It's sort of like fighting. Without blades and fists. Maybe it's more appealing than I first thought.

I'm about to say just that when the boys grab the girls by the waists and toss them in the air. Never mind. I prefer to do the tossing.

"Why don't you dance with Marsa again?" It would thrill her if he did. "Or another girl? I'm sure they'd be pleased to have you."

He smiles, but it doesn't reach his eyes,

which have dimmed. "Of course. Marsa?"

Eagerly, she snatches his hand, and soon they're dancing with the others again. The sight fills me with longing. Probably because it confirms life isn't what it used to be, nor will it ever go back to what it was. That's supposed to be a good thing, though. Why can't I let it be?

I whirl away from them and try to dodge through the crowd, but people stop me often to talk, to congratulate or thank me. I try to get away from them as quickly as possible without being rude. Everyone is most kind; it's just too much. Once I escape, I head up the mountain and to the hall. The walk is invigorating and comforting.

It's dark inside the hall. Empty.

I light the torches hanging on the walls. They do nothing to bring warmth. The space is filled with flickering lights and shadows. I pull out my sword, the fit perfect within my palm. No one to practice with, though. I go through the motions, thrusting, jabbing, and parrying an imaginary foe. It's harder with no one on the receiving end of my blows. I haven't practiced without a partner since I was a Zophasling. Everyone worked hard to help the chosen one.

My muscles bunch with the tension of restraining myself. Until I can't restrain anymore. Too much momentum. I tumble toward the ground and twist my face away. My back slams onto the floor, the pain sharp and stinging.

It's hard and cool beneath me. My muscles ache where they made contact with the ground. But it's not the pain that keeps me from getting up. The pain is minimal. Pain I can handle. The emptiness of the room is what presses into me. What holds me down. The emptiness that will be my life without needing to hunt and kill evil. There will never again be an opponent.

I grip my sword so hard my hand aches. Instead of letting it go, I hug it to me, letting its cool sharpness bring me the only comfort I have left. For the first time I can ever remember, I cry.

Chapter Four

A week has passed since defeating the last evil. I stare at the farmhand, Mirgen, and try to detect a hint of a joke somewhere within the folds of her skin. But I can't find any, so I ask, "You want me to do what?"

Her wrinkles multiply as she laughs, which is a feat. "Don't worry dear. It's not too hard. Merva here's gentle." She pats the cow on the rump. How can she touch the thing? And why does it have a name? "Don't fret over getting close to her."

It's not getting close to it that's the problem. Or at least not the biggest problem. But I have to do this. It's my assigned task for the day, and I won't fail. Even though I can easily fit under the cow several times over and may get stomped on. At least I have the strength and speed to get away. I hope. I ease onto the stool, muscles tense.

"Good. Now take hold of her teats."

She can't be serious. My hands aren't meant for female bovine parts.

"Really, lass, what did you expect you'd be doing?" She gives an encouraging smile. "Go on now. You can do it."

I expected to contribute in another way. But until I find what I'm good at, now that my fighting skills are useless, I get to try everything. Even touching female bovine parts. Lucky me.

Suppressing a grimace, I reach out a hand.

"Kaylyn," Marsa calls out from behind me, "you're needed in the infirmary."

I snap my hand back, fighting a smile. It slides the corners of my lips up anyway, and I don't feel bad about losing. I turn to see Marsa standing next to the gate.

I say, "Guess I'll have to try milking a cow later."

Mirgen shakes her head with a laugh. "Oh, don't bother. It's clear as the twinkling stars it doesn't suit you. I'll let the Aster and Astra know. That strength of yours would have been good when we were bringing the harvest in, but I'm sure we can find something else for you to do."

I grin at her, trying to ignore the fact I'm still struggling to contribute. That I'm useless. "Thank you."

"Anytime."

I rush over to meet Marsa, careful to keep my distance from the cows.

"That was good timing," I say as we head out over the field toward the mountain on which most of the village lives. A village full of people who only do nice, kind, good things. People who don't need looking after. "Is someone really hurt?"

"Yup."

Of course. No need to practice spotting lies anymore. It's no longer a problem needing detecting. One thing to be grateful for. I've never been good at figuring out when someone is untruthful.

"Is it serious?" I ask.

"I don't think so. Brilona was nervous about all the blood, so she sent me for you. It's a head wound. You know how those bleed."

A head wound. My pulse increases. Nurse Brilona rarely treats anything besides illness.

"Did we miss a Malryx?"

"No—it's Felix."

"Oh." I try not to let disappointment color my words. I shouldn't even be feeling that way; it's good that things are better for everyone. I just need to find my new place. "What did he do this time?"

She shrugs. "I didn't get the chance to ask. It's certain to be something entertaining, though."

We climb the stairs to the infirmary. It's one of the lowest houses on the mountainside, keeping it easily accessible with only a few steps to go. Inside, Brilona is frantically grabbing supplies from a shelf. "Praise the night sky. He just keeps bleeding."

She motions to the other corner where a boy about our age lies on a cot, a bloody cloth pressed against his head.

"Hi, Felix." Even at fifteen, his freckles are still bright against his pale skin, unruly red hair untouched by his injury. Just at the sight of him, a grin wants to make itself known. I've missed his company since he left and joined the villagers.

"Did you bring me some wheat berries?" His voice isn't even strained, and he wants to chew gum. He'll be fine.

"Can't say that I did."

Brilona shoves a rag at me and flutters about. "What do I need to do?"

Poor woman. It's a good thing she never came with us to hunt Malryx. "I'll need some hot water."

She bustles off without a word.

"What did you do this time?" I ask Felix as I inspect the wound. Not so bad, exactly what Marsa said. A typical bloody head wound. I should teach Brilona how to handle these better.

"I was trying to see if I could catch a fish with my hands," he says. "Slipped and hit my head on a rock."

I hold in a snicker. "Did you catch one at least?"

"Almost."

"Almost doesn't make a fish." I smile to soften my words. "Not worth the wound then." I press a clean cloth to his head, not letting up on the pressure. "How is it you can handle a sword without killing yourself?"

He gives a sheepish smile. "Swords are

different. I think I've managed to get clumsier since I left the Zophas."

"Maybe you should keep practicing, then."

He nods as if this is the best advice he's ever heard, making me struggle to get the cloth pressed against his wound. Brilona comes back with the hot water, and we get to work while Marsa goes back and forth, coming with clean supplies and taking the old ones away. I show Brilona what I know about the wound and tell her how head injuries behave and what signs mean trouble. The work is familiar. I've enough field experience with wounds like this and much worse. Soon enough, Felix is clean with a bandage on his head.

"As long as it doesn't get infected, you should be fine," I say. "Probably end up with a dashing scar, too."

"Only dashing if the girls don't know how I got it," he says with a boyish smile. "It was easier to get their attention when I was a Zophas."

"I can't bring you back as a Zophas now. I can't even do that for myself. But if you learned to be a little more careful…"

"Who? Me?" His grin widens. "Thanks for fixing me up."

Seems like there's been too much of that gratitude thing going on lately. I punch his shoulder, softly so it won't bother him, but with enough force that he knows I care. "Just paying you back for all those times you kept me entertained instead of letting those long walks get tedious."

We exchange more banter while I clean up. After we wash, Marsa and I head back down the mountain to the hall to get dinner. It's at a sort of halfway point, though still closer to the mountain than the farms.

"Perhaps you could work in the infirmary," Marsa says. "Be a healer."

"Maybe." It would be better than working with the cows, and I'd get to properly utilize my skills. But it doesn't make me happy. There's something missing from the work. It does feel good to help people that are hurt get better but not as good as hunting down evil. Besides, I know little about treating illness and births, which is what healers will mainly be needed for now.

"Do you want to talk about it?"

Everything there is to talk about feels too selfish. Too Malryx-like. "Not now. Sorry, I'm still trying to sort my thoughts out."

"Don't worry about it."

But I will. By the way her mouth tightens, I can tell it's hurt her feelings that I don't want to talk. Seems like whichever choice I make, it's wrong, when all I want to do is what's right. My thoughts have brought us almost to the hall in the center of the village when I spot a gathering of people by the riverbed.

"What's going on down there?"

Marsa looks where I point. "I don't know.

Maybe they're all trying to catch fish with their hands?"

"Hopefully they're more graceful than Felix." I giggle with her, but we quickly smother it. None of the people look happy. Everyone is staring at something with faces drawn. Instinct and curiosity make me switch directions, heading toward the crowd.

Marsa follows, and others from the village trickle after us. Whatever it is, it's bringing a lot of attention. When we're almost there, I finally spot what everyone's staring at. A stranger is sitting on a rock by the riverside. He's thin and pale but well built.

Marsa nudges a boy our age in the crowd with short, curly blonde hair. "Who's that, Tavo?"

"Messenger from Crowin." Tavo's voice wavers. "Weird things have been happening at their village."

"What sort of weird things?" I ask, thinking of the village. I visited it once, a long time ago on one of my first quests for Malryx. It was a small but happy place.

"Animals have been acting as if a predator is about, even when the villagers can't find one. Strange clouds in the forest by them have been growing bigger by the week."

"What type of clouds?" Marsa asks. "The darkness you can only see at the top of the mountain?"

I look toward where I saw the clouds before

41

defeating Morphrac. They can't be seen from the valley, and they never did come and bring rain.

He nods. "Same ones. He said they're even stranger up close. Odd color. Don't ever blow away, only grow thicker and bigger."

Something shifts inside me. Not something good but not entirely bad either. As I finish talking with the others, see Marsa off, and hover around the crowd, the feeling grows. I should only be upset about the situation. The fact that I'm not sends a flash of guilt through me. It mixes with the indescribable feeling but doesn't get rid of it. This sounds similar to reasons we've had to go on a quest. Even if it's not a quest for Malryx, it could be an opportunity to help, which sounds a lot better than milking cows.

⌘

Despite the daylight, the Aster and Astra have gathered those of us who want to hear around the campfire. The messenger, Foley, is in our midst with a bowl of stew. His fourth. I hope he can keep it down. The fire helps take the chill out of the fall air, but after getting my own bowl of stew, I stand in the back. Close enough that I can hear what is said but also to the side where I can read the messenger's expressions.

From the ravenous way he's attacking the

42

food, it's clear something difficult has befallen him. The situation he described, though...I'm not sure what to think of it.

"This isn't something we've encountered before," the Aster says, "but we will do what we can. Is there a specific way your village would like assistance?"

Foley scoops another bite into his mouth before answering. His troubles are bad, but his hunger is still demanding. "I don't know, but if things stay like this, my village won't survive. We'll run out of food. And if it keeps getting worse as it has been, we won't be the only ones."

An iciness that has nothing to do with the temperature shivers through me. The Aster and Astra share a look, and beside me, Jorrin and Marsa lean closer as Foley continues.

"I'm grateful your village has been spared so far, but I don't know if it will stay that way. This has been creeping up for, stars, I don't know how long. We first saw strange plants growing deep in the forest a few years back, but I don't know how long it was a problem before we noticed.

"We didn't think it would bother us, but then it started spreading. Then it spread faster. It hurt our crops, and our animals are trying to flee. We've had to pen them in. Even the ones that usually stay close. The wild animals are disappearing. Our crops were doing well until this year when they just up and withered." His

43

voice grows weaker. "We may need to join your village if something doesn't change soon."

"You and the other villagers are always welcome here. We only wish you needn't leave your homes," the Astra says, her voice reassuring.

Foley sets down his empty bowl. "Do you think you can figure out what's causing these changes and stop it?"

"I don't know," says the Aster. "Without knowing what we're dealing with, we can't know what actions will help or if anything will. Nature doesn't change because of what we want it to do. We will look into the problem, though."

But he's right. What good will looking into it do? Nature has a will of its own. How can we discover what's wrong and fix it?

The Astra says, "Now that our community is no longer devoted to destroying the Malryx, perhaps our new purpose could be to help those towns and villages who have need, starting with yours."

It's a good idea. Not only should we help, but also, giving aid will maybe fill the hollow place inside me. I may not be able to figure out why nature has gone mad around them or how to fix it, but I can figure out a way to assist them. "I'd be willing to lead a group back with Foley to see what we can find out and how we can help."

Foley glances my way for the first time. He doesn't appear so desperate with some food in him. Less pale, at least. The Aster and Astra exchange a look. Both nod. The Astra says, "This would be a good option for you, Kaylyn, and we believe your knowledge will be of great use with the task. We will find others to join you."

Thank goodness they understand me so well.

The Aster turns to Foley. "Would you mind guiding them to your village and answering any questions they may have?"

"I would be happy to. I'm grateful you're willing to aid us. It will put some of the villagers at ease knowing you're looking into it and that we can come here if needed."

Some of the villagers. Others will still be upset that their homes are changing and that they may have to leave. I've seen it before when a Malryx has damaged someone's home or livelihood. Change can be difficult.

"We will get others as soon as we can, then, so you can get back to them," the Astra says.

"I'll go with you." Jorrin's declaration is welcome, yet not unexpected.

"So will I," Marsa says, also welcome and not unexpected. Though I wonder if she would have spoken up if Jorrin had stayed behind. Of course she's ready to move on with her life. I can't blame her for wanting to be wherever he is.

Soon there's a group who have volunteered. All young. All Zophas. Or, really, former

Zophas. Young because that's all that's left of us. Young but strong and accustomed to situations such as these. Or sort of like these.

"It's settled then," the Astra says. "Gather supplies, and you will leave at first light. Vitliruc. May the stars aid you on your quest."

That's that, then. A journey I have no clue what to do with. There's already less of an echo in the hollow space within me.

Chapter Five

Well before sunrise the next morning, we're all ready. We're used to missions coming at all times. Having a full night to prepare is more than enough time; it's a novelty. Judging by the way Marsa and Tavo rub their eyes, some are more used to it than others.

Felix grins at me as he listens to Sosha chattering. The wound on his head is uncovered and scabbed over. He wiggles his eyebrows at me. I'm not the only one eager to be on our way.

Seven of us Zophas are ready with a new sense of purpose. Marsa, Jorrin, Tavo, Felix, Sosha, Azleco, and me. Foley makes eight.

No one sees us off. Good wishes were all given last night. The stars shine bright, and all three moons light our way. A good omen. Foley leads us from town, toward what I'm not sure. I do know the village he described sounded nothing like the little bits I remember.

My pack is familiar and comfortable against my back. More so than the room I'm leaving behind. The journey doesn't meet that same familiarity. I've gone in search of Malryx before. This isn't the same. This situation is serious but in a way we haven't dealt with before. We don't know what we are looking for or how to fix it. Still, it's easier than staying around the village and trying to figure out where my place is. Besides, even if we don't know what to do once in Crowin, we can at least assist the people back to our village. That I can do.

As grateful as I am for something to do, to be helping, I haven't trained for this. You can't fight weather. And though you can slaughter animals, it's not something I like to do unless they're rabid or on their death beds, suffering. Besides, these animals just want to get away. We'll help with them and the people as best we can. I have at least directed crowds of people before.

We're a few miles from home when the sun finally makes its presence known. Its warmth is welcome but not enough to make me take off my cloak. Foley hasn't spoken a word as he leads, but then again, neither have I as I take up the rear. Though I know the Malryx are all gone, I can't help but keep a look out for them. Just as well. There are still wild animals about, just none of the human kind.

Marsa has clung to Jorrin's side all morning. I should be excited for her, and I am, it's only that...I don't even know. Something about their togetherness has me constantly glancing at them and looking away.

Azleco slows down to join me, though he doesn't say a word. He's sixteen and left the

Zophas over a year ago. We never went on any quests together and only practiced with each other a few times. I didn't know him well, but I know him even less now that we haven't been working together. He smiles at me, though, and gives me something to think on other than Marsa and Jorrin. That is more welcome than a best friend right now.

∂∽∾

Two days into our journey, we're almost to the canyon, and moods are growing somber. The sun blinds my eyes. The cool fall air is tempered by the warmth of the sun on my skin. The heat can't last long. Not with the changing seasons.

A sadness grips me as we leave the full warmth of the sun. Its rays lost behind the mountain. We pull out our cloaks but keep walking. The mountain walls on both sides loom over us, angled straight up to the sky, ending high above us. They're made of pale rocks, covered in spots by soft green plants. A few trees have managed to make their homes in the cracks, but I don't know how they survive on the sheer face. More trees heighten the top of the mountain. I feel small and humbled in its grandeur.

As we walk farther into the canyon, boulders, small at first but increasingly larger in size, speckle our path. When we've gone about a mile, we find one almost as big as the hall back home.

"Are any of these going to fall on us?" Felix asks.

I trace his line of sight up the mountaintop. It's growing hard to see the details in the fading light, but the rocks not connected to the mountain are jammed in place with smaller rocks. At least, most of them are.

Foley shrugs. "I've never had a problem with them before." He continues walking. "There's a clearing we can stop at just up ahead."

"Are there any big boulders barely hanging to the mountain side?" Tavo asks.

"We'll be fine."

Not reassuring.

Foley rounds a boulder, moving out of sight. The view that greets me when I follow after him is better than I hoped. There's plenty of space for a camp, wood close by, the river still rushing in the distance, and, best of all, no boulders barely clinging to the canyon wall next to us.

"This is nice," I say.

Foley doesn't respond to my comment but only delivers a dejected, "We can camp here for the night."

I move closer to him as the others start at their tasks. "We'll start early in the morning."

He gives an almost smile and nods.

We quickly get camp set up. The fire burns

hot and bright, the meal cooking over it filling the air with smoke and spices. Once I've done my part, I tell Marsa I'm going to the stream to refill some water skins.

"I can help if you'd like," she says.

"Thanks, but I'll be fine." Truthfully, I'd like a few minutes alone. Since we're not on a quest for Malryx, the only danger lurking should be animals. "Don't wait on me for dinner. I'll be back in a while."

"Enjoy." And her attention is already back on Jorrin.

I quicken my pace until I'm in the trees and then stop to lean against one. The fire is bright enough to light most of their faces and the rock wall behind them even from where I'm standing. My friends and companions, warmed by the flames of light. Felix says something, and everyone laughs, even the somber Foley, though he's the first to stop. Marsa glows with more than just the firelight as she watches Jorrin, whose expression is lost beyond the night.

My chest constricts as I turn away. What is wrong with me?

I cross in the filtered moonlight toward the stream. Now that I'm looking away from the flames, my eyes adjust to the forest around me. The stream is wider than I expected, two moons glowing on its surface.

I refill the skins and set them aside. I reach my Zophasken out to the canyon around me. The others back at camp are bright spots against the otherwise neutral world. And that's all I'll ever feel from now on.

I dip my hands in the cool water and splash the travel dust from my face. It's almost too cold, icy against my skin, but it feels good, clean and pure. I shake my hands dry as best I can and unwind my hair from its usual braided bun. It cascades around me in a sheet of dark brown, adding another shelter from the cold. It is so rarely let down other than to clean it, the long strands seem like they belong to someone else.

One of the spots of light leaves the group and heads toward me. At least I had a few minutes to myself. And then the person is nearing, and I know who it is just by the sheer quietness of his movements. Maybe having one other person with me isn't so bad, even if I don't understand why he's going through the shadows of the forest to find me.

"Hey, Jorrin," I say long before he reaches me.

"I'm never going to sneak up on you, am I?" He sits next to me and dips a finger in the water. He yanks it out and rubs it on his cloak. "How can you stand it? It's freezing."

"Feels good."

"You're crazy."

I stick my tongue out at him. Childish, but he laughs. Friends should always have a chance to laugh together. But then, why does it feel so wrong? The unknown of what we're going into maybe. "Why did you volunteer to come? Don't you like being free from Zophas duties?"

"I've missed... being a Zophas. And, well, it's nice to be with you again." He looks me in the eye before glancing away.

"I've missed being around you, too. The last few months without you were lonelier than I expected," I say.

"Do you mean that?" His expression grows more serious.

"Of course. Being pretty much the last active Zophas wasn't a very jaunty experience. There was less to do and rarely anyone around to do it with. It would have been nice to have a friend around."

"Right." He plunks his fingers back into the water, despite his earlier protest of it being too cold, and holds them there a moment. "I suppose I never thought of it like that. How hard it was on you when everyone slowly got called away for other duties. Maybe if I had thought about it more, I would have hung around more often and not just when you and Showna needed a hand with something."

The urge slams into me to take his now dripping fingers and dry them off with my cloak. "Change your mind about how good the water feels?"

"No."

Huh? That's odd. "Foley's worried."

"He hasn't said anything. At least not to me." Jorrin finally dries his hand on his own cloak and keeps it wrapped up tight.

"It's what he doesn't say and the look he has more and more often. If there's so much worry about the strangeness of the forest and how it's changing them, how much worse will the foliage be with it growing closer to their village? And what if it's not just close to their village by the time we get there, but over it? How will that affect them? How will it affect our jobs?"

"We'll help bring them back home."

"But what if it keeps growing and affects our village too?"

He sighs, a loud, drawn-out sound that carries more weight than he's admitting to. "I don't know."

"None of us do. How can we help if we don't know, Jorrin? How?"

He grabs my hand, warming it with his own despite the chill of the river. Maybe the night air left me cooler than I thought. The touch is so good. I hand him my other palm, too. He turns more fully toward me and presses both of my hands together between his. I shiver but not from cold. The desperation in me has lessened with his touch.

"Just because none of us knows," he says, "doesn't mean we won't be able to help. We'll figure this out. We're smart."

Not smart enough to save Showna. "But we've never done anything like this before."

"The first time you went on a quest for

54

Malryx, you'd never done that either. And you were only ten then."

"That's right. Not long after you caught the squirrel for Marsa and me to pet." I almost forgot how old I was. It seems like fighting has been my whole life. "But I had help and training then, and others with me who had done it before."

"It's going to be fine." His words don't reassure me, but his voice is comforting anyway.

"You're probably right."

"What do you mean, 'probably?'" He grins.

I giggle. What is wrong with me?

He shifts my hands so they're held in one of his, and with his other, he reaches out to grab a lock of my hair. He runs his fingers through it, down to the freed ends near my waist, making my breath catch.

"I didn't know your hair was so long." His voice is even deeper than usual.

"Yeah, I usually keep it up." Why do I sound as breathless as when I just finish a battle?

He weaves his hand more fully into my hair, playing with the locks in a way that leaves my heart fluttering until his fingers brush against my neck. "You should keep it down more often."

I jump to my feet, something about his touch more shocking than the coldness of the water. "We should get back to camp. It's getting really cold out here."

His gaze is intent on me as I quickly braid my hair and pin it back up. I bend to grab the water skins. He reaches to help, our fingers brushing. I pull away and let him take the two water skins closest to him. Once we've got them all, I turn toward the fire and our friends. I can still feel their bright and true Zophasken. Including Marsa's.

"Kaylyn."

"We really should get back. I'm sure dinner is finished by now."

He sighs. "We should talk sometime."

I scuff the toe of my boot along the ground. "Is it urgent?"

"No. I guess not."

"Then maybe it can wait. We really should get back."

As I start off, I hear him mutter, "Not urgent, but important."

Something about his words make my legs move faster. It doesn't take him long to catch up.

"Any ideas of what we should do when we first get to Crowin?" I ask before he can say anything.

"What we always do." His voice is laced with bitterness.

"Of course. What we always do." And my own voice is laced with disappointment, even though I don't fully understand why. "Analyze the situation."

The rest of the walk back is silent. Dinner is already being served. The fire is indeed warming, but I'm still cold. I hand out water skins to their owners. Marsa's last. I feel bad about spending time alone with Jorrin. She should have been the one to do that.

I meet her where she waits by a rock farther from the center of the group. She holds a bowl of soup for me.

"You and Jorrin were gone a long time. Anything interesting?" she asks, my guilt growing with each word.

"We were talking about Crowin." I sit next to her, letting worry replace the guilt. "I'm not sure what to expect or what to do."

She hands me the bowl of food and then pulls a blanket out of her pack. "You'll figure it out."

As she wraps the blanket around my shoulders, I can only hope she's right. "Thank you. And I should have taken you up on your offer to come with me. Then I could have left you alone with Jorrin."

She gives a girlish grin. "That would have been nice." Her grin lessens. I feel like even though we've been around each other more since Morphrac's defeat, we haven't really had a chance to talk. We've been together more, but it feels like less. "Sometimes I almost think…"

I pause eating. "Think what?"

"It's nothing." But the look in her gaze doesn't seem like nothing. "Any cute boys caught your eye yet?"

If not for the weight of the situation on me, I would laugh. I do let her change the topic...for now. She'll talk when she's ready. And maybe I'll talk when I'm ready, too. Whenever I figure out what I even want to talk about. "When would they have had a chance to?"

She grabs a leaf and throws it at me. It floats to the ground several inches from me, and I laugh.

"Go ahead and joke about it for now," she says. "When a man finally captures your heart, you'll realize you're the silly one. Love doesn't need time. It forces its way into your life whether you're prepared for it or not."

"It had better wait to force its way in until later. There's too much to do right now."

She sighs. "I wish it would have waited for me. Jorrin's always busy, like you, even though I've been struck by him. It'll probably be the same for you. Some handsome guy making you swoon even if you haven't got time for it."

I set my empty bowl down. "No time and definitely no swooning."

"Oh, you'll swoon all right."

"You're crazy," I say with a laugh. "Besides, it's not like I'm going to fall here. Who would it be? Tavo or Felix whom I've known my whole life? I could list every embarrassing thing they've ever done. The silent and worried Foley? No, love won't be hitting anytime soon. I'll have to stay on my own two feet so I can keep you on yours."

She shakes her head, but by her smile, I can tell she's pleased with my answer. Zophas girls have left for boys before. Though you're not required to leave if you marry, many seem too occupied with their newfound love and life to have the desire to run around taking down Malryx. I'm sure they'd come if we still needed them, but with little need, more and more have fallen in love and left. And now we all have to leave.

"Do you see those roses?" Marsa says, drawing my attention to a nearby bush. "They are gorgeous."

"They are." Though the beautiful blossom looks a little withered.

"Do you have your—" Marsa bolts upright with a squeal.

I jump toward her, sword in hand. "What is it?"

The others race over, except Foley.

"I'm fine." She puts a hand to her chest and takes a deep breath. "Just fine. Something just brushed against my hand. It startled me."

Azleco snickers. Tavo punches him on the shoulder.

Even after all our years of training together, she really is out of practice. I lower my sword. "What was it?"

"I don't know." She turns from me and makes a sad cooing sound. When she turns back, a small black bird is cupped in her hands.

"I think its wing is injured."

An injured bird caused that shriek? Maybe I should have everyone train when we stop at night. I sheathe my sword. "I don't recognize it. Is it edible?"

Marsa glares at me, then coos at the bird again. No eating it then.

"Its wing needs tending to," she says. "Anyone know how to do that?"

I've tended to all sorts of human injuries but have never done anything for animals.

"I do," Sosha says. She looks the bird over. "Not too bad. I'll fix her up. Then if she can avoid predators for a little while, she will be able to fly again."

Sosha gathers a few things, and then she and Marsa work together to help the bird. I help Azleco and Felix clean the dishes from dinner. By the time we get back, the girls' work on the bird is done, and it's easy enough for my thoughts to turn elsewhere, though I suspect Marsa will have a harder time of it.

We settle for the night, but sleep is not so quick to come. I can't help but think of Jorrin with me down by the stream and Marsa's words of warning about love and swooning. What is the not urgent but important thing he wants to talk to me about? But I shouldn't think of him when the darkness is growing.

Chapter Six

Foley presses us to go farther and farther each day, silent but insistent. The strange clouds in the distance have grown. It could be just because we are closer, but Foley's pushing us harder every hour, which makes me think not.

We left the canyon earlier in the day and entered the forest. The sun's rays filtered by the trees aren't the same as when we first left the village during the day. Night seems to close in sooner in the forest. The moons are harder to make out and provide less illumination to help us travel at night. It's past time to make camp, but I don't have the heart to tell Foley. We've set up camp in dark, awkward places before; we can do it again if it gives him peace that we will reach Crowin sooner.

We trudge on for another two hours in the dark, the pace growing slower as we take time to make out branches and rocks. The forest is strangely muted, except for what little noise we make. It's the quietness that has me on edge. My Zophasken can sense nothing amiss, but silence like this doesn't come without something bad brewing.

I make my way past Felix and Sosha to

where Foley is leading us. He looks at me but says nothing. I can feel the others watching me from behind. Probably hoping I'll ask him to stop. And I'm going to. It's just that I hate to disrupt his journey.

"Did you see that?" Foley asks.

"See what?" Only I see it before he responds. "Is that a squirrel?"

"Not like any squirrel I've ever seen."

And he's right. Its fur is molted with blackness. I'm ready to point it out to the others when it scampers off. "That was strange."

"It's the type of thing going on around here," Foley says.

My foot comes down lower than I was expecting, wetness seeping into my boot. "What is this?"

Foley gives me a hand and helps me back to dry land. "It gets a bit marshy ahead."

"Ahead?" I shake my boot and carefully keep disgust from my voice. Wet feet are the worst. "I think it's here."

"You're right." He pauses. "We should probably stop."

I put a hand on his shoulder. "We'll help them. I promise we will."

He nods but doesn't answer. The others are watching, Jorrin and Marsa included. She's going to tease me later about falling in love, but I learned a long time ago that a small amount of physical contact can help those with low spirits. I motion for them to set up camp on dry ground.

They quickly get to work. With their hands and ears busy, I ask Foley, "Do you want to talk about it?"

"It's nothing." But he doesn't move.

I wait. And it doesn't take long.

"Laynori."

A name. Now we're getting somewhere. "What about her?"

"I'm going to marry her. Was supposed to be married already, but all this has changed so much. We kept hoping things would get better if we waited, so we could have the wedding we wanted." He grips his hands together and looks out into the darkness over the marsh. "When I was chosen to go get help, she begged me to marry her before I left, but I told her there wasn't time and things could still get better. I put her off. The woman I love, and I put her off. I never should have."

Marsa would have been the better choice to talk to him. She'd know what to say. I haven't a clue. "I'm sure she'll be there waiting for you. And you can wed her first thing so you won't be parted, no matter how things go."

He closes his eyes. "I'm sure you're right." He turns toward where the others are making camp. "We should help."

"Yes, but..." He looks at me, and again, I feel like I should send him to Marsa. Instead, I bravely say, "If you ever want to talk about it, I'm here."

"Thanks."

"You'll have to introduce me to her."

His lips widens into the first real smile I've seen from him. "I will. She's not much like you. I don't think she's ever worn breeches, but she has a good heart like you."

We all have good hearts now. I don't bother correcting him, though. "I look forward to it."

We help roll out sleeping pads. It's easy and familiar even in the dark. There's little talking as we settle down for the night. I almost mention the conversation with Foley to Marsa, but my awkwardness worked somehow, and I don't want to break his confidence. The next morning, we eat and pack up with the same pensive reserve.

The marshland is darker than I expected, filled with clumps of grass, dark bushes, and trees. The distance holds the threatening clouds, dark and unmoving. A chill runs through me just looking at them, growing worse the closer we get. No wonder Foley is in such a state.

I look out across the expanse and whisper to him, "We'll get to her."

"Hopefully today," he replies, no hope sparking his words.

"Then push us hard so you can go marry your true love."

My words light something within him that wasn't there before. He nods and sets a harsh pace through the wetlands. For a while I try to keep close by, in case he wants to talk, but soon give up. Not only am I not the best person for the job, but his haste is making him flick mud everywhere, including on me. There's enough grime without adding splatters from him.

I let Tavo and Azleco pass. Felix gives me a charming grin and promptly slips to the ground landing on his knees. I rush to help him up. He shoos me away with a quiet laugh.

"Don't worry about me. I'm fine." The bottom half of his pants is wet and muddy, but the rest of him really does look fine.

"You are the luckiest clumsy person alive."

He wiggles his eyebrows at me and then gets moving again, hurrying to catch up with the others. They must not have heard him fall. It probably sounded too similar to Foley treading.

Sosha and Marsa both have grins on their lips as they motion to let me join them. I shake my head. "I'm going to take the rear."

They nod and hurry along. Jorrin is a ways back. Not so far that he can't see everyone but farther than I would expect of him. Almost like he's not part of the group. I suddenly don't know whether I should wait for him or go now. I should have joined Marsa and Sosha. It shouldn't be that difficult of a choice. Doing what's best for everyone usually comes so naturally. As long as there's no talk of love, that is.

My indecision decides for me. Jorrin catches up to me and asks, "Everything all right?"

I shrug. Not really. "I guess." I gesture at

the mud splatter on the bottom of my cloak to emphasize how things could be better. "Foley seems like a really great guy, but he's not used to moving like a Zophas."

Jorrin smiles. "No, I don't suppose he is."

The others are getting farther away. I start walking after them, Jorrin falling in line with my steps.

"So you think he's great?" he asks.

"Yes. Look how well he's led us and answered any questions we've had. I know he doesn't talk a lot, but you can tell how much he cares."

"What does he do that shows he cares?"

"Look at the pace he's set this whole time. If he didn't care for his fellow villagers, he wouldn't be pushing us so hard."

"He cares about the villagers?" His voice is lighter.

"Yes?" His questioning of it makes me wonder if I guessed something wrong.

"You're right. It's easy to see how much he cares." My hesitance dissipates at the agreement. He continues, "Do you think he cares about other things?

"What do you mean?" Is the swamp making him a little addled? I'm kind of thinking so.

"It seemed like you two were having an intense conversation last night. I thought that maybe there was something more to it."

Ah. That explains it. I think. Maybe? "There is. Kind of. He's engaged to one of the village girls. He's worried about her."

"That I can understand."

I look ahead at Marsa chatting quietly with Sosha. He would understand about being worried over a girl. At least she wants him to. I don't know if he's realized it yet. And she's so ready for him to. The question is, would she want me to help? She knows I'm not good at talking about these things, but I feel like I should do something. Best friends take care of each other, after all, whether watching their friend's back for wayward swords or helping with…guys.

I try to steady my feet as best I can in the muck as we go. "What do you think about Marsa?"

He looks away. I don't know what to make of the action or his silence. We walk, trying to avoid the worst of the wet and mud. And still he says nothing. I'd much rather be protecting Marsa's back with a sword. Thrusting into some attacking Malryx is so much easier than helping her catch a husband.

Finally, he says in a voice that's darkened, "Marsa is a nice girl. You're a good friend to her."

I spend the next few hours walking by his side, trying to determine how that makes me feel and just what exactly it means.

The marsh slowly gives way to the forest, blocking the ever-looming clouds from view. Within the forest, night comes sooner. It's dark and cold, but I don't even attempt to suggest we stop. We keep plowing along, with torches lit and held high to help avoid any obstacles.

The trees begin to thin until we step from the forest. One of the moons above us brightens the sky. Partway across it and the village, the sky is heavy with clouds that look like they're bruising my beautiful night sky. Dark purples and greens, tinged with black. Just looking at it makes me feel as if the stars have abandoned us, even though they are shining.

The forest surrounding the village thickens as it stretches to the other side. The moonlight barely reaches the trees straight across from us. Tall, thick, dark trees. Maybe it's the lack of moonlight, it's hard to tell from this far away, but they don't look natural. Too sharp and jagged. Whatever is going on, I hope we don't have to go in there.

As we head down the slope toward the village, we're more silent than we've been except when sleeping. It doesn't take long to reach the first house, but unlike when someone comes to my home village, no one comes out to greet us. There's not a person in sight. When we went on quests in the past, someone always greeted us, unless we got there too late. Are we too late?

"Where is everyone?" I whisper.

Foley looks around and then up at the clouds we're almost under now. "I don't know. The hall, maybe."

His assessment has me more on edge. I slink after him, constantly checking the area around us. I stretch out my Zophasken and rest my hand on my sword. Everything is like it should be behind us, but where we're about to head to, where the line of clouds starts, everything is tinged with darkness. I've never felt anything like it.

All the huts are closed up tight, the windows dark. Pens are broken and empty. There's no sign of life, except for us. By unspoken agreement, we all stop before we cross under the clouds. I stretch my Zophasken farther, into the darkness under those clouds. It makes me cringe and pull back. Nature has never felt like that before. After a moment, I force myself to push past the feeling. Not too far into it, there's a group of light. I pull my Zophasken back, tight within me.

"I think there are some people up ahead, a little to the right."

Foley nods. "That's the hall."

But no one moves. I don't want to enter something that made my Zophasken shiver in such a fashion.

I pretend I'm an extension of my sword, all hard metal, stiff and dangerous, and stalk forward. My body doesn't feel different as I move under the clouds, if it can really be called that. But the area brushing against my Zophasken makes me prickle and keep up my guard.

The others follow. There's a faint charred scent to the air, not like the comforting smell of fire but like someone burnt their hair and the stench hasn't cleared. There are no flames or evidence of something burning within eyesight.

Everything else seems the same as before, but then we pass a house with its door splintered and cracked, like someone or something was desperate to get out. Or in. Soon after, we pass an animal pen that is unlike any I've ever seen. I may not know a lot about animals, but I've seen enough pens to know this one is different. It is almost completely covered with logs, thick and sturdy. The walls are at least as tall as me.

In a subdued voice, Sosha asks, "What's going on with that animal corral?"

"Like I said, the animals have been trying to get away," Foley replies. "It helps keep the last of our sheep from escaping."

"You need something so big to keep them from that?"

"Some jumped out of the fenced plot. One even escaped after we built the walls higher."

I eye the enclosure with a new appreciation. Those animals must really be scared to jump out of something so tall. As I take in the structure, a glint from a gap between two logs catches my eye. Something is watching us.

A sheep, I think. Its nose is marked with a

jagged white line down the side, the rest of it so dark it mixes with the shadows. Its gaze continues to follow us. The feel of it has me struggling not to pull out my sword as we move past.

We stop at the biggest building. I let my Zophasken out just enough to know this is where the good is coming from, like it's supposed to be. The place is silent though, without a hint of animals or people. Not even the endless bubbly noise of children. Still, their light is shining bright against my power. Perhaps they're all sleeping? But even that doesn't seem right.

Foley presses the handle and pushes the door, but nothing happens. He shoves harder, but it still doesn't budge. As he knocks, I scan the area around us to make sure no one is creeping up on us from behind. Shuffles come from inside.

"Who's there?" a male voice calls out.

"It's me. Foley. I've come back with help."

There's a clank from the other side of the door; then it bursts open. A girl rushes out, wrapping her arms around Foley. Laynori. Who else would greet him like this?

"You're back!" She covers his face with kisses as she starts to cry. "I was so worried."

He lifts her up, pulling her close to him. "Hush now, I'm fine. Nothing happened to me, and I've brought people to help."

At his words, she finally realizes we're

71

standing behind him. "I hope they can do something. Let's get inside quick."

Foley allows her to pull him into the hall while he asks, "What's the urgency?"

The rest of us follow. I try to come in last, but Jorrin waves me forward. With a final check around us, and seeing nothing, I step into the hall. I stop just inside with Jorrin tight on my boots. The door is slammed shut, a thick bar placed across it.

The hall is wide, deep, and full of about thirty of forty silent people with the same pale faces that Foley had when he came to our village. Tables and chairs in one corner are full of people staring at us. Another corner has blankets on the floor with more people, including children, staring at us. Even more people stand right in front of us with solemn faces.

Foley's actually quite handsome with the glow he's taken on. "This is Laynori. My betrothed." He quickly introduces all of us, though his gaze never leaves Laynori. Finally, his expression sombers a bit. "What is going on? Why are you all in here?"

And moon take it all, why is it so quiet?

"The animals have changed," Laynori says. "They've been attacking us, even when we try to feed them. Attacking each other." She rests a hand on his arm and says quietly, "A sheep got your dog."

Foley's face goes slack. "A sheep? Lucky

72

was supposed to protect you, not succumb to a sheep. I should have taken him with me."

"I'm sorry." She wraps her thin arms around his frame.

Jorrin leans closer to me, his breath warming my neck. "What would make a sheep do something like that?"

I don't have an answer, though I realize I'm leaning closer to him. The room is cold with tension and silence. Though he's not touching me, Jorrin's warmth is welcome, especially after the chill of the clouds.

The silence doesn't last long. The people begin asking us questions. The first one opens the floodgates, and others quickly follow until they overlap. I can hardly grasp what they're asking.

"What's happening to our village?"

"What are you going to do?"

"Did you bring any adults?"

"How are you going to stop this?"

Stop it? I still don't know what it is, let alone how to deal with it. The noise grates on my skull. This is nothing like defending a village from Malryx. What have we gotten ourselves into?

෴

I sip out of one of the cups Laynori passed out to each of us when she brought a small portion of food. It tastes wrong, murky, like old fish were soaking in it. I try not to make a face and set my cup on the table.

"It's tasted like that for a while," Foley says.

Not some local custom then. It's a relief that I don't have to act as though I like it, except it means there is no fresh water to scrounge for. No wonder he was so desperate for a drink at our village. At least I still have some in my water skin, but it won't last long.

"Tastes like what?" Felix asks.

Before I can answer, he takes a big swig, then promptly spits it across the table all over Tavo.

"Are you mad?" Tavo asks, attempting to brush the droplets off him.

"Ugh, no. This is just disgusting."

Tavo rolls his eyes and takes the cloth Felix offers him.

Gross. But I can't blame Tavo. I wanted to do the same thing. I pick up my bowl, hoping the food will help me rid my mouth of the taste. The small bowl is half full of some sort of broth and bits of vegetables. I take a bite and inwardly cringe. Though it's not as bad as the straight water, it's still quite foul. Only now it has vegetables and a few herbs to help with the flavor.

"Sorry," Foley says. "We didn't have a harvest this year. We only have the last bits we stored from before."

"Don't worry about it." I take a big bite to

prove I mean it. The villagers are sharing what little food they have with us. Even though they don't have much, I won't insult them by declining their offerings. Besides, food is life. When you get it, you don't refuse.

Laynori sits on a chair next to Foley. I can't help but notice her bowl of food holds even less than ours do.

"Thank you for the meal," Jorrin tells her.

"Our pleasure. I'm only sorry it's not our usual fare. I'm afraid this is a sad example compared to what we ate when times were better."

"Don't worry about it," Marsa says. "We understand."

Once dinner is finished, Foley leaves our group with Laynori. The other villagers keep a respectful distance. I feel as though I should ask them something, but questions like, "Where was the Malryx last spotted?" and "Has anyone in your village been tainted by the Malryx?" aren't relevant. What else is there to ask?

The villagers know very little anyway, only what Foley has already told us. Instead, I try to focus on what we can do. The forest is where this all started. Even without being able to see it, an oppressive rage feels like it's drifting from that direction. There has to be something we can do about it.

"I think we need to go into the forest," I say to the other Zophas. The silence returns just as quickly, this time with long, trepid looks. Like me, they've trained to fight Malryx, not invisible threats. I push on. "If we explore it, perhaps we could discover the problem."

"Has the water affected your brain?" Sosha asks.

"No, it hasn't," Jorrin says, reprimanding but soft. "What did you think we were going to do? Come here, look at the people, and then leave? She's right. The villagers don't know what's going on, and they've been here a lot longer than we have. They haven't learned anything by living here. How could we by simply visiting? They didn't know to look for a problem when the forest first started changing. We're going to have to go in if we want to figure it out."

His words are supportive, but I almost wish he would have come up with a different option. A better one. The feeling of the forest is so heavy and potent from a distance. How bad will it be when we're actually in it?

"Sorry I lashed out. It's just terrifying," Sosha replies.

"I don't want to go in there," Marsa says.

Me neither.

"Me neither," Tavo says, voicing my thought.

Azleco asks, "Do you really think we'll be able to find out anything by going in there?"

I force out more confidence than I feel. "Of course."

"What if it's just like here?" Tavo asks.

"No answers anywhere but without buildings to protect us. What if there are animals that attack us like they did Foley's dog?"

The word "attack" pulls out my real confidence. "We know how to handle ourselves in a fight."

"Not in a situation like this," Sosha mutters.

"Should we go right now?" Azleco asks.

The question has perfect timing. It's something I can handle. "We should start at first break of light."

"Do they even get light here?" Tavo asks.

Marsa scolds him with a look. "Tomorrow is good. Be grateful we're not going tonight."

Despite her words, everyone still looks nervous instead of relieved at the extra time. So I say what we always said before facing Malryx.

"Anyone who doesn't wish to participate doesn't have to. We only need those who are willing to join us."

Everyone looks a little relieved at my statement, but if they don't all show up in the morning, I'll never again call myself a Zophas. We always do what's required, even if we don't want to. We know what's right.

While the others are busy talking, I lean over to Jorrin and Marsa. "Would you two please talk to the villagers? Foley, maybe, or another they consider a leader? Foley should be able to guide them back to our village. They need to go. Even if we fix this, they won't have enough food to last the winter. Make sure they know they will be welcome and that they will have help repairing their village once the problem is found and taken care of."

Might as well give them something to work on. Kill two Malryx with one swing. It will give Marsa more time with Jorrin, and it will help the villagers.

Jorrin nods, but Marsa asks, "Are we really going to be able to find the problem and take care of it?"

"I don't know." Dread scrapes through me, but I don't let it taint my facade.

She nods as if it was the answer she expected. Together, she and Jorrin leave. They don't go to Foley, though. I guess his conversation with Laynori looks too intimate to break up. Jorrin and Marsa find another to discuss things with. I lie back, resting against my chair, trying not to think about how long my Zophasken is going to be curled inside me, frightened to leave.

My thoughts are interrupted by a loud whooping. I turn to see what the excitement is about. Foley and Laynori are beaming in the midst of the crowd.

A man hollers, "There's going to be a wedding tonight."

I smile. At least something is going as it should.

᠀᠍᠀

A ladder at the back of the hall leads to the roof where they hold the wedding. There are a few tables here, and the space is mostly lit by torches. The festive mood is dampened by the reality of the situation. The already-darkened sky is an unfathomable black, weighty with whatever is going on out there. When we awake, will the whole sky be covered?

For such gloomy circumstances, the wedding is a surprisingly cheery one. I join the wedding circle as I should, though it's hard to focus.

Foley beams as he whispers his promises to Laynori. He seems to be making up for all that stress and worry he put himself through before. What must it be like to feel for someone so deeply?

Once Laynori and Foley whisper their promises to each other, they begin to dance. To sway and jump in time, reminding me how much I thought dancing was almost like fighting before. It's enough to make me wish I had taken Jorrin up on his offer. To find out what it is like for myself. But of course that will never be. At least not with Jorrin.

The thought has me so out of sorts. I jump when the wedding cheer sounds. The newlyweds have finished their dance and started their new life together. I shout for joy with the others celebrating. But no matter how happy I am that Foley has found this for himself, I can't bring myself to yell as loud as I want. Too much is hanging over us for that.

I keep to myself as the ceremony turns to the social portion. I should be sharing in the joy, but everything just is so off. The threat is looming, and the job that needs doing is impossible. No way to ignore it. Worse, no way to fix it.

As I wander, I spot Jorrin and Marsa. My first instinct is to join them, but even through the thin black haze that surrounds us, I can tell their bodies are close. They're not touching but closer than mere friends should be. As close as friends turning to lovers.

I hurry away, the darkness pounding at me almost as hard as my power clenches inside.

Chapter Seven

The next morning, each and every one of our group has their packs on ready to go. It's dusky out, though the sun should have risen half an hour ago. The villagers are awake as well. At least the ones who are still in the hall with us, which is most of them.

A few, very few, left last night to go to their own homes when the newlyweds did. How much longer can they live like this? Not long, if the little bit of food they gave us last night and packed this morning to take on the journey is any indication. The food and water that could mean the difference between us living and dying.

It could be the same for them. They need to take Marsa and Jorrin's advice and not wait long to leave. Hopefully we'll be with them, but looking at the forest with trees like a cloud-covered midnight sky and branches as sharp as my sword, I'm not sure.

The villagers are silent as they watch. They have already shared warnings about the forest and expressed gratitude to us for going anyway. What else is there to say? I wish there was something. Their silent sendoff is almost as eerie as the forest. It would be better if they didn't see us off at all.

Jorrin pulls up the bar and opens the door. After checking the area outside, he leads the way. The others follow one by one until I'm left alone with the villagers. I don't tarry and neither do they, closing the door behind me and slamming down the bar.

As I follow the others, my legs shake in a way they never have before. The cacophony of these new feelings is as unwelcome as it is unsettling.

The morning is darker than I expected. I suppose the villagers had lit the hall with so many torches that even when dawn came I had the expectation of it being bright out. Or maybe it seems darker because now I'm heading to the even dimmer forest.

Judging by the sun hazed out above the horizon, it's later than we thought. It's easy to stare straight at the sun through the clouds. Except it's hard to call those things clouds. Other than hanging in the sky above us, they're nothing like normal ones. Instead of blocking or filtering the light, these have distorted it. The golden, warming power of the sun is maimed into a blotted green that covers the entire village and leaves my skin chilled.

I walk faster, keeping my Zophasken nestled tightly inside. Though we're together, it's quiet and lonely as we leave. The villagers' fear outweighs their gratitude. And it is contagious. Though there's nothing out here yet. Nothing at all. Not even a sound. It's worse than if there were screaming and howling or vicious animals attacking.

The forest looms before us. Jorrin halts before going in, and everyone gathers around him. There's no slow buildup of foliage. No way to gradually work our way in. Just a straight line of tightly-knit plants. Trees with trunks bigger than any I've ever seen, covered with black, spiked bark. If it weren't for the gloom and the spikes, this would be a beautiful forest.

Right now, though, none of us want to enter its deadly presence.

"Wait," Laynori calls out. "Wait just a moment."

She runs to us, Foley not far behind. She takes a moment to catch her breath. "I just wanted to say thank you. I know this is difficult, but I appreciate what you are doing for our people."

"And I do as well," Foley says.

"We're happy to help," Jorrin says.

Laynori hands him a bundle. "It's not much, but it's something."

He opens it to find a thick blanket, better than any we brought with us. With the chill permeating us since we got under the cloud, I don't know if it's even thick enough, but it will help.

"Thank you. It's beautiful," I say.

"Hopefully we'll be seeing you soon, but don't wait for us. If you need to leave, just go."

"We will," Foley says.

They back up but don't return to the shelter, waiting instead for us to depart.

No one moves. Finally, I step forward and enter the forest first. Only a few strides in, and it's already darker. I can't see Laynori and Foley. The thick foliage is tinged black. The faint light that was shining outside struggles to get past it.

The others follow me in. It doesn't take long for it to become completely dark. I can't decide if it's the clouds or the leaves growing denser. Neither one is visible enough to discern. We all stop to light our torches before continuing on.

"I don't like it in here," Sosha says.

"Me either," Felix says. "And my Zophasken likes it even less."

"You feel it too?" I ask.

Everyone nods.

"Worst thing I've ever felt," Azleco says.

That I can agree to. "Let's get this done as fast as we can, then."

I hold a torch in one hand, my sword in the other. Gaze sharp. Ears straining for any sound other than the faint shuffle of our moving through the forest. Dry twigs crack beneath our feet. No animals chitter about.

The air has a rancid stench to it, worse than the burnt-hair smell from yesterday. Rancid mixed with vomit and decay. I thought I'd get used to the scent eventually, but if anything, it seems to get worse as we trudge on. There's nothing but dark, putrid trees and the six of us.

As bad as the darkness and stench are, what I'm feeling is even worse. I want to be comforted that the others feel it too, but it's so foul, I don't want it myself and would never wish it on another. I keep my Zophasken wrapped tightly inside me. Whenever I try to let it out to help me sense the world around me, it's as if I'm brushing it against Malkine, the Malryx's power, an evil stain that is all around trying to taint me.

We walk for hours, heading deeper into the forest. If I wasn't so used to gauging time, I would have lost track of it long ago. Every hour seems longer than the last. Each step gets darker and fouler. Even the light of our torches dims in the gloom until they barely seem to flicker. It's difficult to make out anything on the ground or around us. When we reach a spot where the trees give way to a clearing, I can't make myself push on.

"Why did you stop?" Azleco asks.

Because this place is wrong. "I don't know where to go. Everything has looked the same for the last several hours." Or the whole time we've been in here really. "I'm not sure we're still headed east. If it weren't for this clearing being new, I'd think we were going in circles."

"We're lost?" Sosha asks. "I've never been

lost before."

Neither have I.

Tavo asks, "Should we split up?"

When there's this many of us and we come to a problem, we always split up. Always. It's easier to cover more ground and find information or people that would otherwise take two or three times as long. Even the youngest of us knows how to fight.

"We should stick together," I say. Here, none of us even knows what we are looking for, let alone what to do if we figure it out. Besides, I want as many of them by me as I can. "We don't want to make things worse by being lost from each other."

The tension eases from them, though it doesn't leave entirely. As we huddle close together, it's still hinted at by the way they carry themselves, shoulders slouched and faces drawn. We're all pressed and shoved out of the familiar; we're allowed some stress.

"Maybe we should camp here for the night," Marsa says.

Is it even nighttime? Seems like it should be the next day, but time is difficult to gauge in here. This is as good a spot as any other to stop, though there's nothing good about it, other than a little room to stretch out. It's better than continuing to wander around aimlessly. Though I suppose that's what we'll do when we start again, unless we come up with a better plan.

"It does feel late," I say.

"And I'm hungry," Felix says.

Agreements sound from all around. But somehow staying here feels like a bad idea. Deep in my gut, I feel it. This place... there's something wrong with it. Not wrong like the rest of the forest but something stronger. Something that reaches deep inside me and twists. The thing that sapped my strength and didn't let me go on walking.

But there's nothing here. Nothing different than what we've seen in the entire forest. I trust my instincts, but I don't know what to do about it other than be even more vigilant.

"It's settled, then. Set up camp here. Everyone get to work readying us for the break, but no one goes out of sight without a buddy. Even then, stay close." Perhaps not safe enough, but it's not like we have options. "We'll eat and take shifts through the night."

"Yes, ma'am," they say.

The salutation is strange directed at me. It was always used for Showna.

Everyone gets to their tasks, and I help where needed, but really there's not much to do. Other than constantly scanning what I can see of the forest to figure out where a Malryx is hiding, watching, waiting for the right moment to attack. No matter how many times I tell myself there are none left, my Zophasken won't let me believe it.

The feeling of evil is all around us. The only good is coming from those with me.

There's none of the neutrality I'm accustomed to. I'm not used to such overpowering sensations.

Dinner is a somber affair. The fire is piled high with wood. Despite the plentiful, dry fuel, the flames don't burn bright. Just like our torches seem overpowered by the darkness in the air, so does the fire. It's like whatever makes it so dark suffocates any light. Though I'm not made of light, I feel close to suffocating myself.

And for the first time ever, I can't eat. I've always been able to force myself to when the occasion calls for it. I know I'll need the energy. Plus, our food is rationed. I can't waste it. Yet, I can't eat it either. And by the untouched plates of others, I'm not the only one.

"Tavo and Felix," I say, "could you see about saving what you can from dinner? I don't think anyone is hungry. Maybe we can eat it for breakfast."

"Of course."

They jump up and quickly gather everything. Everyone looks grateful not to have to force themselves to eat.

"Let's get settled for the night. I'll take first watch." There's no way I could sleep anyway.

There are no objections. The silent forest continues to loom around us as everyone pulls out their blankets and tries to find a patch of ground big enough to stretch out on.

Finally, I can't stand it anymore. I put my pack on and sit against a tree. With my pack between us, the sharp edges can't cut me, and having my back against something makes me feel more normal. Though it doesn't really fix the underlying problem. As long as we're in this forest, I don't think there's any way to do that.

Without a word, everyone dutifully hunkers down and closes their eyes. None of them look at ease doing it, though. Five little lights struggling to sleep in the forest.

After a while, several of them start to breathe deeper, sleep taking them in. It's still distant to me, which is good since I'm on watch. I don't understand how they can succumb.

Time passes slowly and agonizingly. Threats lurk all around, but I can't watch them all. The harder I try, the more I feel like I'm missing something. Usually I rely on my Zophasken, but with it tightly wrapped inside me, I'm blind. I finally give in and see if anyone is awake to help.

I tread softly, trying not to wake those who have managed to fall asleep, which seems to be everyone. Though they said the forest bothered them, maybe it's not affecting them the same as it is me.

I stop where Marsa lay down. She's always been able to sleep no matter the circumstances, but I still didn't think she'd be able to in a place like this. We've all been trained to sleep on command, but I've never been good at it. Her soft snore is a familiar comfort from the many times we've gone on quests together. I can't bring myself to disturb her now. If I can't find anyone else awake, I'll ask her. Otherwise I'd rather let her rest.

I pick my way through the sleeping forms, careful not to step on anyone. Felix is hugging his blanket rather than having it draped over him. Sosha is drooling. They're all asleep until I come to Jorrin. I don't even have to check to see if he's awake. He's already watching me, his green eyes clear and alert.

"I can't watch everywhere by myself," I whisper.

He nods and slips from his blanket without a word. After he's folded it and rested it on his bag, he turns and says, "We could stand back to back in the middle."

"Should we go farther out? Separate?"

"I think we'll be fine in the middle. With the fire so low, it won't distract us, and we'll probably be able to see the entire camp best from there anyway."

"Right."

We step over Azleco, the only person between us and the fire, and stand in the middle of the clearing. All of that doesn't take long, but I almost wish it would. I'm suddenly apprehensive, though in a different way than the forest is making me. I spin away from Jorrin and try not to be so overly aware of his presence.

He turns away from me and presses our backs together. Immediately, it's easier to breathe. My muscles relax like they haven't since we arrived at the village. He's warm, and it transfers to me along my frame. He's only a little taller than me. Years ago, I used to be the tall one. Now my shoulder is about an inch below his.

I let my gaze roam from one side of the camp to the other, carefully checking all that I can see and trying to peer past the dark to what I can't. Jorrin is doing the same. With him at my back, camp is more secure. Safer. But evil still lurks.

After some time, Jorrin whispers, "Do you think something is out there?"

"I don't know. It seems like it, but I can't see or hear anything. The forest seems abandoned, as if the animals ran away, like the villagers said. But there's still a threat here." And I don't know where it is or how to stop it. I'm failing. "When we've gone on quests before, I could sense where the threat was coming from. Now there's nothing. Except it's not nothing. The nothing feels like something. Which sounds like nonsense."

"Not nonsense. I know what you mean."

"Do you feel it, too?" I ask.

"I feel it."

I'm not alone. It's coming from everywhere; it's not only my fear making me think so. Something evil is all around. Except where Jorrin's back touches my own. That spot is cleaner, clearer, crisper than any other. The light of the others is welcome, but with him, it's more than his Zophasken I sense. It's just him. Warm and powerful. Comforting.

Marsa would appreciate it. But I'm kind of appreciating it, too. Appreciating him. And I really can't sleep, and she clearly can. It feels like I'm breaking her trust, though. And breaking my own vow to help her marry him. But it's not like I haven't stood watch with Jorrin numerous times.

This is different. I'm overly aware of him.

Uncertain how to deal with this new awareness, I force my thoughts elsewhere. To what we should really be focusing on. "This darkness all around us. It's strange."

He sighs. "I know what you mean. I've never experienced anything like it before."

Successful change of subject. "Do you think Showna ever did?"

"If she did, I think she would have told us. It's so different. Not just different, but wrong." His voice is quiet, skimming across the air as he moves his head to scan the area like I do.

"Does it feel like the Malkine to you? Like evil's power is everywhere?"

"It does." His voice is somber.

The darkness is filled with a silence so thick and unnatural, I want to draw my sword and slice through it. I don't want to think what that could mean. But it's the whole reason we are here. To figure it out, this slimy, oily thing that sticks to my Zophasken like tar. My power burns even as I keep it tightly wrapped inside me. Malryx no longer exist. Except no one told this forest.

Or maybe it knows.

My stomach churns. I'm grateful I didn't eat anything at dinner tonight. If my thought is right, if this grew as Morphrac's and every other Malryx's death happened, are they connected? Did ridding the world of all evil cause an issue none of us could have foreseen? And what exactly is the problem? What is going on here? The evil feeling surrounding the Malryx always felt like this entire forest does. Could it be— Could it possibly be that without people to be evil, nature is turning evil?

A memory comes to me. The Astra cutting the vine when I was younger. Her saying it needed cut back to thrive.

That it needed conflict.

I don't want it to be so. And yet… "Do you think it's a coincidence that this problem has grown as we killed off the Malryx? That it's getting increasingly worse now that I executed Morphrac? And maybe Morphrac knew what was going on and that's why he was so easy to beat?"

He's silent for entirely too long. Finally he shifts, his arm brushing mine. "The timing fits perfectly."

"The world needs evil as much as it needs good." The statement burns my mouth.

"I think you have just discovered the problem."

My heart is heavy with those words. What have I done by ridding the world of evil? "What am I going to do about it?"

"You mean we," Jorrin replies. "What are *we* going to do about it."

I wish I could see his face right now. See if he really means it. If it's true, I've caused much of the problem and sent the balance spiraling out of control with Morphrac's death. I know Jorrin is willing to make it so I don't have to fight this on my own, but how can he assist? I don't even know what to do, let alone how to have him help me.

Jorrin says, "I don't know what we can do about it. Fighting Malryx I understood, but this —" He waves his hand at the forest round about us. "How do you fight nature?"

"You can't."

Chapter Eight

The next morning, at least we think it's the next morning as it's impossible to ascertain in the dark, we eat breakfast. Or last night's dinner. Azleco and Tavo are able to force it down this morning, but I only manage a few sips of the foul water. Mostly, I keep a sharp lookout.

Marsa sits down next to me. "You never woke me to watch."

And I should be stifling back a yawn, but I'm still too awake. "Jorrin and I watched all night. I don't think I could have slept. How did you manage to?"

She shrugs. "It was easy to sleep because I knew you were guarding over us."

My eyes sting, and I turn my face away. I blink a few times. It's probably the lack of sleep getting to me. Or the truth of how I feel toward Jorrin when she is so trusting of me.

"What's the plan for today?" she asks.

I swallow past the tightening of my throat. Jorrin and I never did decide on a course of action. We were both too stunned by the realization of the problem. I still feel too stunned. What are we going to do? "I don't know."

The forest is still quiet and dark save for what we've brought to it. Nothing has moved except us. Not a wisp of a breeze. Nothing that is, except the distinct impression of evil pressing in on us. And it's my fault.

I've killed seventeen Malryx, most within the last few months, and I killed the very last one. Everything that has happened, driving animals away, making them and the weather act strange, making crops fail to grow, the darkness, I didn't just aid in happening, but I sped up the process. My stomach is sour.

I rush behind the tree we've designated for girls' use and heave in the dark. The little bit of water I have in my stomach is quickly gone, but it's not enough to rid my body of the nausea. My hands are clammy, and my body flashes with heat. I heave again, but nothing comes.

A faint light from one of our torches comes up behind me. I silently groan. Someone puts a hand on my back.

"Are you well? Is there something I can do?" Marsa asks.

There's no good response. Instead of answering, I straighten and accept the water skin she's holding out to me. The water is clean and pure. Cold on my tongue. Fresh. It must be from the tiny store we have left from filling up before we got to Crowin. As much as I appreciate it, right now I'm not sure I deserve it. "Thank you."

"Is there anything else I can do?"

I almost rest my head against the tree, stopping just in time from having it cut my forehead. There's no way to let up from any of the stress for even a moment. Anything she can do? Not only am I to blame for her mother's death and us being in this situation, but I think I have feelings for the boy she's loved forever. The one I vowed to help her marry.

"Nothing. There's nothing you can do." My voice sounds feeble, but she doesn't comment. She just waits patiently for me. I sigh, and we round the tree back to camp.

With the light of the fire dancing on his face, Jorrin glances at me as we return but doesn't say a word. His gaze on me is intense, as if he's trying to find out what's wrong just by looking at me. He's probably just waiting for a clear view of Marsa.

If I keep telling myself that enough, maybe it will be true.

Everyone sits around with their things packed up, torches in hand. Sosha and Azleco also have their swords out. I haven't put mine away since I first pulled it out yesterday. Marsa and I join the others, and she finds a spot in the middle, right where she belongs.

When no one does anything, Tavo says, "Now what? We keep wandering around the forest?"

"I don't think that will help," I say. Going deeper into the forest isn't going to bring more answers. I think I stumbled onto the answer last night, and from the look in Jorrin's eye, he agrees. So what now? We just go back to the village and tell them to leave their homes? That we've failed? I've never failed before. Not once. But it would seem in my succeeding to kill the Malryx, I've caused much greater harm.

"We should head back," I say, trying to drag my thoughts back to the issue at hand. "Jorrin and I think we know what's wrong. We'll explain on the way out."

Not that explaining will undo the damage, but maybe one of them will have an idea. They all look skeptical but grab their packs without question. It isn't more than a moment before everyone is ready to go. I should get my torch out, but there's one thing stopping me. I don't know where to go. Nothing looks familiar, not even the spot we entered the clearing from. My chest clenches. How can I be this lost?

"Um…does anyone know where we came in at?"

They look around the clearing, their faces filling with the same helpless, lost feeling consuming me.

"Great. Just great," Sosha says. "We're lost."

"And now we get to die in this freaky forest. Wonderful." Tavo huffs and shifts his weight. Next to him, Marsa looks as if she's trying to hide her fear and failing miserably. I'm failing her miserably. I'm failing them all.

"Complaining won't help," Jorrin says. "Why don't we relax a little and see if we can come up with a way to get us out of here?"

"Not like we can relax in here," Felix says.

I wholeheartedly agree.

Packs go back on the ground, along with some of our group. Others choose to stand. Felix goes from tree to tree, careful not to touch them. He inspects them as if they will tell him the way out. Hopefully, he doesn't trip and land face first in one. Jorrin and Marsa converse in quiet voices I can't hear. At least that is going as it should. No one looks my way.

"What's the problem anyway?" Tavo asks. "What's wrong with this forest?"

The focus suddenly shifts to me. Do I tell them? I want to take the coward's way out and let Jorrin explain. Better than letting them know how much I've ruined things. I hate answering questions anyway, and this is even worse. But watching Felix examine the trees gives me an idea. Maybe there is something I can do. And it provides a perfectly legitimate excuse for not explaining it myself.

"Jorrin, would you please explain it to them? There's something I want to do."

He gives me a curious glance and comes over to me, Marsa following after him. He asks, "Do you have a plan?"

I don't want to get his hopes up. I don't know if it will work. I've never heard anything about it before. "It's probably nothing, but I'll let you know if I discover otherwise."

"Do you want help?" Marsa asks.

More than words can say, but there's nothing she can do. "Thank you, but I need to do this myself. Jorrin, would you please let them know what's going on?"

He looks like he wants to say something else but shakes his head. "Of course."

They turn away from me. I waste no time sitting next to the closest tree, facing it. My pack is still on my back, and my sword in my hand, but I move my free hand toward the tree. Sending fireballs will only destroy it. What if I could use my Zophasken to heal it instead? The gloom pushes in on me as my skin brushes against the inky bark.

"Ouch!" My hand stings.

I yank it back and see the jagged edges cut into my skin. Blood wells to the surface. I look closer at the bark. It's even worse than I first thought. Has it gotten worse? The jagged pieces of bark each have several tiny knife-like pieces protruding from them. Maybe this isn't going to be as painless as I thought. Even if it doesn't work, I'm going to come away damaged, but a few cuts are nothing if I can gain anything.

Gingerly, I put my hand back on the bark, this time ignoring the stinging in my hand when the bark cuts against my skin.

I close my eyes and let myself become accustomed to the tree. Jorrin's voice is calm and comforting in the background. I hope the others don't hate me when he's done talking to them. But if this can fix it, it will at least help with their anger. I let his voice sooth me as I continue.

My Zophasken quivers when I try to push it out. It wants nothing to do with the world around it, but the need is too great. I give it a giant push. It obeys but cringes while it moves. It brushes against the tree, curling back when it encounters the vile power. The tree is even worse than the air. I shove my Zophasken forward. It shakes against the darkness. The tree's core is infested with evil as sinister as any I've ever met. It's like Morphrac's but in a tree form I can't fight.

Maybe I can do something better than fighting it.

It's never like this in nature. Plants rest on the brink of neutrality. Occasionally, something like a healing plant will be a little good or something like a poisonous plant will be a little evil. Never is there such raw evil in a plant. It makes me dizzy just to have my Zophasken mingling with it. But to see if this will work, I need to go further. I take a deep, calming breath.

"My powers are yours." And I push my Zophasken to the tree.

"What did she say?" Jorrin's voice comes from somewhere behind me. "Kaylyn, wait!"

But I ignore him. I have to know if this works. If I can fix it. I thrust my powers, letting my goodness flow to the tree. Or trying to let it flow in. It's like trying to fit a sword into a hilt that's too small. My power keeps slipping to the sides, never merging with the tree.

It has to work. It has to. I fight harder. My Zophasken seems to sense what I'm trying to do and rails against the tree, searching for any way it can slip in. The evil in the tree bends and warps under my shoving. Dodging me, moving away from my power or brushing it aside.

Something sounds in my ear, but I'm so focused I can't understand it. My power pulses in waves. If I can just move past the barrier, the tree has to let me in. It wants to be rid of this unnatural evil inside of it. I know it does. I push harder, straining my power with everything I can.

The tree still doesn't give. I pull my power back and ready myself to spring it all at once at the tree. My head spins.

Jorrin yells, "Kaylyn, stop!"

I let out all my bunched up power, slamming it against the tree. Instead of breaking through, my power crashes against the tree and falls away. It's not working.

Then something happens I don't expect. The tree's evil rushes back at me, shoving itself into me. My power retreats, aching.

My eyes flutter open. The already darkened world around me spins and manages to darken further. Jorrin's face is all I can see. But soon, even that is gone, swallowed up by a numbing blackness.

Chapter Nine

Something soft and warm touches my cheek. It smells of clean woods and the faint metallic scent of swords. It's calming against the darkness that lingers. Why it's lingering I can't remember, but I know I want it gone. I nuzzle toward the warmth. It nuzzles back. I open my eyes. Jorrin. His hand is on my cheek. My pulse speeds up. I start to smile. Until Marsa peeks over his shoulder. The tree and darkness rush back to me, my Zophasken groaning with the memory.

"Did it work?" I ask.

Jorrin jerks his hand away from me. "Whatever idiocy you were attempting failed."

I groan and sit up.

"Take it slowly," Marsa says.

I glance over at the offending tree. Sure enough, it's as dark as before. Maybe even darker, though I don't know how that could be possible. When I reach out to check it with my Zophasken, my power doesn't respond. It stays huddled in a ball inside me. My power is not responding, and the tree is at least as dark as before. My stomach falls.

"I thought it might work," I say.

Jorrin huffs. "Giving your Zophasken to something not meant to have it in the first place? How did that seem like a good idea? At least you're not dead from that lunatic move."

My heart skips a beat. "Dead?"

"Yes, Kaylyn. Dead. Completely gone from us all." His fists bunch. "Didn't you ever pay attention to anything we were taught about our Zophasken other than how to fight with it?"

Um…no. "I thought the tree would be affected like a person."

"Shine it all! Sometimes you are so ignorant." He jumps up, moves past the others and paces to the other side of the clearing. It seems even darker without him next to me, even if he was scolding me.

Marsa takes his place, the torch in her hand not enough to replace the light from Jorrin, even in his angry state. "He's just worried about you. We all were."

I choke back the lump in my throat. "I thought it would work. I thought I could fix it."

Marsa gives me a sad smile. "I know, but it doesn't work like that. Plants aren't meant to be meddled with."

"What about the animals? Would it work with them?"

"They're part of nature. Nature can't be tempered with."

"It would have been a good idea if it wasn't for that, though," Felix says, standing behind Marsa.

"Thanks for at least trying," Azleco says.

No plants. No animals. Only people. And if it's only people, then there's no other course. Everything my life has been about, I have to undo. I have to bring the Malryx back.

Chapter Ten

I clear my face of emotion, not wanting to give them an idea of what I'm thinking. They'd try to stop me. I take a deep breath. "Any ideas how to get back to the village? We should see what we can do to help."

"The villagers will have to evacuate, if what Jorrin told us is true," Sosha says. "But the Aster and Astra already said they could come live by us, so we know where to take them."

At least evacuations are something we're used to. But how many other towns and villages will be affected by this? They can't all seek refuge with us. There isn't enough room or supplies for us all to live on. And what if the evil continues to spread until it reaches home? We'll not only have to figure out how to help everyone else but ourselves as well. We won't have the means to do what's needed.

I sit straighter. Did that tree just sway? Of course not. My head aches. Marsa must sense it, because she digs into her pack and pulls out some willow bark and a water skin.

"Thank you."

"Rest a minute." She takes out supplies to clean my cuts. At least I used my left hand.

Can't injure my sword hand.

"I'm fine." My Zophasken is already starting to relax a little. I stand and gather my pack, pretending my head isn't aching.

"No one ever did say if they figured a way out of here," Tavo says.

"I may have thought of a way. If Kaylyn can do it." Marsa says.

I don't like the sound of that. "What is it?"

"If you can stretch your Zophasken far enough, you should be able to sense people's light back in the village. You could use that to lead us back."

"It's a good idea." But the thought of leaving myself open to that much evil while searching for the villagers leaves me cringing. My power doesn't like the thought either and pulls itself tighter inside me. I don't know if I can force it out with the damage I just did to it. It would be hard enough, even without the recent injury.

Jorrin stops his pacing to watch me. Everyone is watching me. I owe it to them, no matter how it makes me feel. I will my power to do this, no matter how horrid it feels. "I can try. I don't know if I'll be able to reach that far."

"If you can't reach, we can give you more of our Zophasken," Felix says.

"None of you have more to give." Though if I'm going to bring the Malryx back, someone, probably several someones, are going to have to give it up. The thought makes me ill. I can't do

107

that to any of them. Not again.

"We have more," Marsa insists.

"It'll be fine." Or it had better be because there's no changing my mind on the matter. "Just need a moment. I'll see if I can feel them."

I meditate a few minutes. My power is a little more at ease but still dreading what I'm about to make it do. I push my Zophasken outward. I let it fly from me. I don't want to slowly brush up against all the evil in this forest. The slow torture of it seems worse than quickly getting it over with. The darkness scratches and burns against my power. Grates against it. Makes it recoil. I press it on, searching in all directions for any bit of good I can use to lead us out.

I'm surprised how far my power goes. It's gone far before, but it seems like it's darting through the evil barbs farther than I thought it capable of. Or maybe it just feels farther when every inch is agony. Though as far as it can go, still there's no hint of what I search for.

"Did you find them yet?" Tavo asks.

I ignore him, not ready to let them know I've failed. Again. Instead, I focus my Zophasken in one direction at a time; there's more to stretch out this way. I try straight ahead of me first. There's nothing but evil as far as I can reach. I try to my right, and there's still nothing. Nothing.

Maybe a different tactic will work better. I focus in on my left, letting my power flow out

108

through the evil, trying to ignore the barbs that scratch against my power. It spans out, searching. Still no light. I repeat the process behind me and in front of me. I don't want to fail. I can't let myself fail.

I shove it out again, this time to my right. My Zophasken struggles against the burning. It stretches out as far as it can. I want it back safe inside me, but there's no one else to try. If I fail now, there will be nothing left.

Everywhere I touch, there's nothing but the icy burning of evil. It doesn't matter how much I want it. I've failed. I press my lips together to keep my failure buried inside. I'm about to pull it back in when something flickers, tiny and faint, but something definitely not evil. I turn my body toward it and concentrate harder. Something's there. I don't know who, but I found some faint bit of good.

I smile. "I've got something." I push away any doubts that it might not be the village. It's the only chance we've got. Even if it's not them, it's someone. "Let's go while I can still find them."

"Do you need to rest more first?" Felix asks. "I hate to say it, but you look awful."

"Thanks." I wrinkle my nose at him, even though I'm sure it's true.

"He's right," Jorrin says. I guess he's speaking to me again, even if it's only to agree that I look bad. "It's a long journey. You should rest first."

"There's no resting in here. I want out."

Azleco hands me a torch. "We'll follow you."

With the torch held high in one hand and my sword tight in the other, I lead them away from the clearing and toward the flickering bit of good. It's so far. It took us a day to get here. How long will it take to get back? I'm anxious to reach it, to not have to hold my power out toward it and be chafed by all the evil.

"Stay close. I'm going to try and go out faster than we came in."

And get my Zophasken back inside me where it's safe from whatever is out there.

Everyone lines up behind me. Azleco first then Sosha, Marsa, Tavo, and Felix, with Jorrin watching our backs. I'm grateful he's there. Ready. We haven't had any problems, so I shouldn't be so worried. But instead of making me relax, the lack of problems is making me tense, like something is building, waiting to unleash its wrath on us. And touching so much evil intensifies the feeling.

I try to keep focused on my power. Not on the pain everywhere else, but the flickering goodness in the distance. So, so distant. It doesn't feel like we will ever make it there. How did we get this far from them? Or does it only seem far because of all the evil grating against my Zophasken?

I don't remember the trek taking so long before. Which is all wrong. Before we were stumbling through the forest blindly. Now we're being lead directly where we need to go. At least I hope I'm following the right thing. About what I think is an hour later, it's still the same size. At least I don't have to strain through as much evil to find it.

After hours of traveling, its brightness has been slowly increasing. So slowly. That's why it doesn't seem to get closer. It's such slow, tortuous progress it's as if nothing is happening. Still, its steady light is the only thing that keeps my feet going. My sword is slack against my side. The torch does nothing but make my arm exhausted. I don't remember the last time I struggled with something physically.

"Do you need a break?" Azleco asks, his hushed voice for my ears alone.

I almost stop, but I'm afraid I won't be able to get myself going again. Instead, I slow and hold my torch out to him. "I'll be fine. This is doing me little good, though."

He sheathes his sword and grabs the torch from me. "We can take a break."

I shake my head and march on. The light is still getting brighter, but the pain and the burning cold are like daggers repeatedly stabbing my Zophasken.

Someone trips behind me. I scan the forest ahead, but of course see nothing but black so dark it coats me. I'm missing something. I know I am. I turn to see who fell. Four torch lights behind me. Felix.

"Are you all right?" I call out to him.

He quickly gets to his feet, juggling his sword and torch in one hand while brushing off his knees with Marsa's help. He gives me a shy grin. "I'm fine. You know me."

"Can we keep going, or do you need a break?" Part of me wants him to take a break, but the rest of me fears it. We need to get out. Now.

"I'm good to continue going."

I turn, a smile teasing my lips. Things feel a little more normal if Felix is stumbling over something. Life can't be all bad.

We continue on, following the light. A few steps later, there's the halting sound of someone tripping again. I roll my eyes and turn. "We can really stop and take a break if yo—"

Sosha's on the ground. A chill spreads through me. She's one of the most graceful people I know. She flashes out her hand and grabs her sword off the ground. It must have fallen when she did. She darts back to her feet.

"Are you all right?"

Her face is pale, eyes wide. She looks spooked, but she nods.

"Are you sure? We can take a break if needed." Please say no. My urge to run from the forest is growing stronger.

Her voice is shaky. "I'd rather keep going."

Good. "Let me know if you change your mind. That goes for anyone."

At the back, Jorrin's doing a superb job of

scanning for trouble, but there's nothing there. Like there hasn't been since we entered the woods. No one says a word as I continue on, my pace even faster than before. They keep up with me. It feels as if we're running from something, but nothing's there except the evil knifing into me.

Nothing there.

My heart beats faster.

Nothing.

My legs stretch out longer.

Nothing.

My breathing becomes shallow. Uncontrolled.

Nothing.

My foot finds its next step, steady and sure. Then suddenly something moves right where my foot is trying to land. Something else grabs hold of my ankle, making me lose my balance. I twist as I fall, not only so I can keep my sword but so I can see my leg.

I barely notice my fall to the ground. Everything is focused on my ankle. In the faint light, there's something dark wrapped around it. Azleco leans his torchlight forward. My ankle is trapped by something dark and serrated.

A branch with all its spiny bark is tight around me.

My power zips back inside me. I have an urge to scream, but I contain the noise. Several members of my group aren't as quiet with their emotions.

I wiggle my foot to try to free it. The ragged bark cuts into me. I hiss. I pull my sword back to try and cut it off.

"Wait." Marsa steps forward. "Let me. I can get a better angle."

I keep my grip on my sword but put it back down. She nears and doesn't hesitate to lift her sword and bring it down on the branch. Pain jolts through me, the branch cutting deeper into my ankle.

"Are you all right?" Marsa asks.

Just peachy. "Fine. Just finish it."

I lower my head as if I'm watching what she's doing, but really, I'm closing my eyes so I don't have to see. The pain is getting worse, as if the tree is attempting to claw into me. Trying to take my foot off. A scream bubbles up in my throat, trying desperately to escape.

I can't take more of this, but I have to. The forest makes a crackling protest. There's a jolt against my ankle again. Once. Twice. Three times in quick succession, but I still have to clench my teeth to keep from calling out.

But then I'm free, the branch breaking loose from around me. As I lift my foot, the world around me changes. A shiver of leaves blows in the wind, softly at first, but with increasing ferocity.

Blood drips from my ankle.

"I'm so sorry," Marsa says, voice tiny.

"It wasn't you." Stupid tree.

"We need to clean that," Sosha says.

114

"Not now." I jump to my feet, ignoring the shooting pains in my ankle, and take my torch back from Azleco. "Grab a hold of the person in front of you. We're going as fast as we can. Yell if you need something."

My Zophasken jumps from me. The pain doesn't seem as bad with the burst of energy. My power zips around until I find the light, and I run after it, pushing past the agony shooting up my leg.

Marsa clings to my pack, just as the others are hopefully clinging to each other. The shaking of the trees grows louder, and now I don't just hear it. I can see it through the faint light of my torch. The branches are whipping back and forth. The wind seems to be coming from them and not the air. We have to get out of here.

I put forth another burst of speed. A branch whips across my face. My cheek stings. Blood runs down both it and my ankle, but still I run.

Suddenly, Marsa screams, "Tavo!"

I slow, but Tavo yells, "I'm fine. Go."

So I keep moving. Branches tear at me faster now. I hold my torch in front of my face and run as fast as I dare. It's hard to move fast when I can barely see in front of me. Something strikes my shoulder. The pain is searing.

A limb moves toward me, thick enough it shouldn't be so malleable, but still it comes. Once it's in range, I bring my sword down toward it. It darts out of the way, wraps around my waist, and yanks me into the air.

This time, I don't hold back my scream. It pierces through the night air as I soar through it, cutting branches and leaves. The limb around my waist pulls me back and throws me. I almost drop my sword, but I don't want it to hit one of the others. Instead, I pull my legs and head into myself, pointing my sword away from me. I beg the stars that it won't hit one of my friends. That I survive the landing.

The branches beat at me, cutting at me as I pass, but also slowing me. I don't know whether to be grateful or resentful. One slices deep across my leg, just above my knee. Everything aches and burns as I slam against a branch and then fall to another and another and smack in a pile on the ground.

I grip my torch and sword tightly, and I swing them around, trying to chop or burn anything attacking.

A groan escapes me. The forest howls like a giant pack of angry wolves. No. Like a giant pack of angry Malryx.

I roll onto my back, curl my legs toward me, and keep my torch high, swinging it at anything that comes near me.

The others are calling, but with the angry howling, there's no way to tell how close they are. I stay curled up, assessing the damage as the branches lash at me. Nothing feels broken, but it seems as if I'm bleeding everywhere. The gashes on my ankle and leg sting the worst. I don't know if I'll be able to run. Forget that. I don't know if I can move.

"She's over here," Jorrin's voice calls out.

A moment later, something shields me from the whipping branches.

"Kaylyn?" Jorrin's voice is frantic. His hands move across me, gentle, but probing for injuries. He touches the wound on my leg.

I groan.

"Thank the stars!" Jorrin says.

Footsteps sound. Wind howls.

"Is she alive?" Felix asks.

"She's fine." Jorrin scoops me up in his arms. "You have to tell us where to go, Kaylyn."

I mumble. My words still aren't working, but my Zophasken is strong, reaching for the light that isn't much farther now, straining for it, like it knows how close to death we are. I point toward the one spot of hope. A branch slices my finger. I scream and pull it back into me. Jorrin is already on the move.

He trips, and I know we're both going down. As angry as these trees are, I don't know if either of us will get back up. Something yanks him backward. I slide forward, but he yanks me back to him.

Azleco appears, a branch whipping across his face. He yells, "Let me know if I get off course."

He moves ahead of us, swinging his sword and torch. Felix and Tavo move next to Jorrin's sides, doing the same with their swords and torches. It looks like a tight fit, but it seems to be working. The lashing-out branches stay clear of the torches.

We run. Or rather, they run, and I point whenever they get off course. Jorrin yells directions to Azleco. We must make it. My head is clearing.

"The others?" I finally manage to say.

"Behind us," Jorrin says.

The shaking of the leaves increases, becoming a deafening roar. The branches still seem to fear the light but try to dart past it anyway. One reaches past Azleco and stabs Jorrin in the shoulder. He grunts.

I climb out of his arms against his weak protest. Leaves fly at us, so we can barely see each other. Felix holds the torch up to the limb. It wiggles and starts to smoke. It jerks away from Jorrin. Dark liquid seeps from his wound. Though I've seen it before, this time something about sight of his life blood dripping out of him makes me feel faint.

I rip the bottom of my shirt and press the cloth against his wound. "Hold it here."

I turn and try to take a step forward. My leg buckles, but there's no time for weakness. I ignore the pain and yell, "Move!"

We dodge obstacles as a group. Branches and leaves fly at us. A leaf slices the skin on my forehead. One more spot from which to lose my life force. The light has never seemed so close

118

or so far.

The roar somehow manages to get louder, but the branches stabbing at us are gone. It's still dark, but something has changed.

No flying branches. The air is still oppressive. Dark. But more open. I swing my torch around. The trees are gone.

Once we're a bit farther, I yell, "We're out of the forest."

Everyone halts, swings their torches around us to make sure, and then relaxes to take a breath.

"Then where's the village?" Tavo asks.

Chapter Eleven

"This is where Kaylyn led us. It must be in front of us," Sosha says. "It's just too dark to see it. It must be night."

I did lead them, but it's just as dark as when we were in the forest. The darkness must be moving quicker if there's no light. Unless it's night, but even then we'd be able to see the stars and a moon or two far off in the distance.

"The clouds must be moving faster and becoming thicker if this is the village," Marsa says.

"They are. Much too fast. I'm glad we're all safe from the forest, but it's not enough. We need to get to the villagers and get home." I want to wrap my arms around her in relief. She made it out safe, but we're still not out of danger.

She doesn't share my hesitations, pulling me into a hug. It makes my wounds cringe, but I hug her back anyway. She says, "I thought you were going to die."

"You know me. Even a tree throwing me around isn't enough to put me down."

When a hiss escapes me, she finally pulls back. "You're bleeding."

"I think we all are." Though my voice does crack with pain. I just have to push past it for long enough.

"Let's get moving, then." Jorrin's voice is weaker than its usual strong self. We all have to push past our frailness.

"Something's not right," I say. "Let's go see what's here."

"Can you keep walking?" Jorrin asks.

"Can you keep bleeding?" The torn cloth over his wound is already dark with blood. I hate to think what my own cuts look like. "We can assess our injuries when we're safer."

We start moving again, and our pace quickens as we move to find the village. It's hard to be hopeful when we've just been attacked by a forest and there's no light.

The first house comes up so quickly, we almost run into it. I swing my torch away from it so it doesn't catch fire. Though this pitiful thing would probably take a lot of work to get a fire going.

"We're here." Marsa's voice is filled with relief.

Everyone starts talking excitedly. Jorrin gives me a nod like he knew I'd find it all along.

The light is getting stronger, but everything is so much more oppressive than before. "Everyone must still be in the hall. Let's go."

We make our way through the village, one house at a time. I'm no longer leading. After our fight in the forest, I'm tense. I keep behind the line of my eager friends, limping along, trying to keep an eye out. Though for what, I'm not sure. There weren't any trees in the village that I remember, so we shouldn't be attacked by another one. We shouldn't have been attacked in the first place. Evil trees that can attack. I wouldn't believe it if one hadn't thrown me through the air.

The others' excited chatter stops. I step up to see why. We've reached the hall. It stands before us, much as it did when we arrived two days ago. At least, I think it was two days. Only this time, the door has been reinforced.

"What happened?" asks Sosha, panicked.

"Apparently things got worse," Jorrin says.

Azleco knocks on the door and calls out, "We're back."

There's a clang as the bar is lifted, and the door squeaks open. The slim amount of light coming from inside hurts my eyes, even though it's blocked by Foley.

"Hurry." Foley's voice is gruff, barely heard above the din from the forest.

We file in, blinking against the light. Foley slams the door closed behind us and bars it. The howling forest is muted but not silent.

As soon as I'm sure we're safe, at least for the moment, I collapse. Marsa catches me, and I let my weight move from my bad leg to her.

"We need medical help," Marsa says.

The room goes fuzzy. Voices faded and muffled. Someone lifts me and lays me on something soft. Hands prod at me.

"Jorrin," I slur. "Jorrin needs help first."

"I've only got a little poke," he says. "I'm not the one bleeding to death."

"You're bleeding. I'm…" Fine. But my mouth won't say the word.

The prodding continues, followed by pressure. Unconsciousness swallows me.

Chapter Twelve

There's a sound, but I can't bolt to my feet. I can't even open my eyes. Malryx are attacking, and I can't defend. My breathing becomes panicked, until I remember there are no Malryx left. So then where am I, and why can't I move?

"Kaylyn?" Marsa. "You're safe. I'm here. We're all here, and we're all fine. You're going to be all right."

But Jorrin's not. It comes back to me in a rush. He was stabbed by a tree. A tree, for moon's sake!

I force my eyes open. A group of them hover worriedly next to me, and sure enough, Jorrin is a little paler than usual but otherwise looks well enough. He's wearing a new shirt; the telltale thickening on his muscular left shoulder is certain to be a bandage.

I try to speak, but it comes out as a sad squawk.

Marsa grabs a water skin. There's a large gash in her cheek. "Sorry. We don't have any good water left."

She helps me drink. The stuff isn't as vile when I'm so parched I can't even talk.

"Careful," Marsa says. "Granny did a good job bandaging your shoulder, but you don't want to take any chances."

What more of a chance can we take after that trip in the forest? Still, for her sake I try to be more cautious as I drink. When I'm finished, I glance at Granny. She's weathered but dignified with her white hair and wrinkles. I ask Marsa, "Everyone is all right?"

"Yes."

I nod. "How long was I out?"

"Not long," Felix says. "Maybe an hour."

An hour that we can't afford to lose. "We need to leave. Now."

I try to sit up, but Marsa puts a hand on my shoulder and pushes me back down. "You need to rest and heal."

"Do I have any serious injuries?" I ask, though I already know the answer.

Her lips purse. "No. You lost a lot of blood, though, and have a lot of open wounds."

"So I'm only a little weaker from blood loss from cuts and scratches."

Her grip on my shoulder tightens. "We had to put a few stitches in your leg. You need to be careful so they don't tear."

Felix winces. Jorrin stays silent, his brooding expression never varying.

"If he's fine, then so am I." Gently, but firmly, I brush her hand off me and sit up. The room tilts but quickly rights itself. I don't push it by standing up. Yet. "Has anyone talked to the villagers?"

Their gazes all turn toward the ground.

"It's been an hour," I say. "What have you been doing?"

"Trying to make sure you weren't dead," Jorrin snaps.

"Clearly, I'm fine."

Felix holds his hands up in the air. "Don't look at me. I'm trying to get used to not being the one everyone's hovering over."

A small smile slips out, but I quickly rein it back in. "Truly, I'm fine, but none of us will be if we don't leave. Did they say if it's night?"

None of them say anything. I try not to roll my eyes. Can't fault them too much for being worried over me. I'm still concerned enough that I don't stand. I try to ease the harshness from my tone. They're trying to help as best they can. Now, I just need to get their focus on something else.

"Azleco, would you please get one of the villagers. Preferably Foley."

He looks only too happy to be given an errand instead of staying here with me.

I sigh and rest my aching head on my hands, cradling it. "I feel like I lost a fight with a mad tree."

"You did," Marsa says. Her voice turns admiring. "Jorrin, however, seems to have won the fight."

"I got stabbed in the shoulder," he retorts. "I don't call that winning."

"You have fewer injuries than the rest of us."

"Only because Azleco and Felix were protecting us," he says. "Besides, no one else got stabbed."

"Any other wounds besides minor cuts?" I ask, wanting to put some distance between whatever this thing is, hovering, waiting to strike.

"Nope," Marsa replies. "The worst of it is the two of you right here."

"Good," I say and turn to Jorrin. "How did you find me in the forest?"

"My power is growing, enough that I could stretch it out to find you." He shrugs like it's nothing.

But it's something. If it hadn't happened, I don't know what those trees would have done to me or what would have happened to the rest of them. I want to take his hand. Instead, I say, "Thank you."

I want to look at him but focus on the throbbing of my head. How long until it calms down enough that I can think?

"You wanted to talk to me?" Foley asks.

I raise my head just enough to look at him and motion to the chair Felix abandoned. Once Foley's sitting, I ask, "Is it night?"

"Almost midnight, but it's been this dark all day. The cloud cover moved over the rest of the village after you left."

Expected, but not what I wanted to hear.

"And the reinforcement on the door?"

His discomfort grows. "Something tried to get in a few hours ago. Don't know what, but it sounded unpleasant."

"What made it go away?"

"I don't know, but once we were sure it was gone, we reinforced the door. It's come back twice but not for a while."

The new information sinks in for a moment, before I decide it hasn't changed a thing. If anything, it makes leaving all the more imperative. "We need to leave. Now."

"I was afraid of that." He brushes his hand across the floorboards as if they're the finest silk. "It's hard to leave your home knowing you'll probably never come back."

I have no response, but Marsa puts a hand on his arm.

He stands. "I'll let the others know. How soon are we leaving?"

"Three hours," I say.

"Tell them to pack only the essentials," Jorrin says. "We're going to be moving fast."

"We'll be ready."

I bury my face back in my hands. The throbbing is lessening, but a tired ache is replacing it. Food is put in front of me. I give my thanks and shove it down my throat knowing I need it. When was the last time I took such a beating? I don't think there was a last time.

"You two both need sleep," Marsa says.

I want to argue, but she's right. Besides, I haven't the energy for it. I roll back down on the cot, and, almost asleep, mumble, "Wake me in two hours."

৵৵

I jolt awake. My internal clock says it's been about two and a half hours. Why did no one wake me? The villagers are moving about frantically, packing what little they have and rounding up their children. The bustle of their movements carries with it a hushed but harsh worry. Nothing appears wrong, except the fact that they have to go and their concern for what's out there.

I sit up slowly, but no dizziness comes. More sleep would help, but it's not bad. The gash in my leg and my wounded ankle are tender, as are the other cuts, but nothing that should hamper me too much.

After standing and still not feeling dizzy, I go in search of the reason no one woke me. I find my fellow Zophas in front of the door surrounded by villagers. They are patiently trying to work something out with the villagers, but by the stress lines forming, whatever it is, it's taking its toll.

"What's going on?" I ask.

Marsa huffs. "Some of the villagers want to get things from their houses. We told them they should leave their stuff behind. We don't know

129

what's out there, and we don't have time to get it."

She's right, but I can't help but remember the way Foley looked before I fell asleep. The way his fingers gripped so lovingly at something as simple as the floor. They're losing everything.

I turn toward the group. "You can go on three conditions. You move quickly. We are leaving in half an hour, no exceptions. You grab only what you can carry. No one else will be doing it for you. And you take one of us with you."

The villagers' faces ease, relaxing, though their gazes still dart toward the door. Marsa is miffed, her chin jutted out just enough to say so. Well, she doesn't have to understand, just help, and she has a good heart. She'll do it.

I arrange the villagers and Zophas as quickly as I can, making sure no one is missed and that we don't waste time we don't have. When everyone is ready, I put on my stern face and say, "Let's go."

We hurry the villagers along into the darkness with torches that give off little light. The forest is silent. After the noise and anger from before, it's more nerve wracking.

They're quick to get their things, just as agreed. We're all making our way back when we hear a shuffle to the side of us.

"Did another villager follow us out of the hall?" Sosha asks.

"I don't know," I say. "I don't think so. I can't feel anyone else."

Felix yells, "Hello? Anyone there?"

"Quiet!" Jorrin says.

And I know why he's suddenly become snappish. A slithering of evil races across the back of me. I twirl around, my bad leg trying to give out, the flames of my torch whooshing. How can evil slither across evil?

"Get in the hall," I demand, sword ready.

There's scraping behind me, louder this time.

"It's us," Azleco yells from in front of me toward the hall. "We're back."

Hopefully, the rest are close to him. There's movement across my Zophasken again. I try to track it but can't detect anything further. What is going on? This is like nothing I've felt before. The door opens, and the villagers move in first.

"Faster," I say.

But no matter how fast both Granny and Marsa try to move, the woman just isn't as agile as she once was. Laynori stays close to the two of them, trying to help Granny as well. Her steps widen, determination crossing her gaze as Marsa takes her by an elbow

Tavo is still standing by me. "What's the hur—"

His words are lost in a strange, frantic growl. I whirl toward him. Something is jumping at him. Felix flies toward him, jumping in front of Tavo before he's attacked. The

131

creature and Felix go down, away from where my torch lights up.

"No!"

It takes me a moment to find him, and by the time I do, whatever attacked him is gone. Or at least staying out of the small range of my torchlight. I still feel it moving around me.

"Tavo, help him in." Felix has deep gashes with blood flowing from them, and I can tell he's going to need help. A lot of help. "Jorrin, I nee—"

I don't have to finish; he's already moving to help.

"Get in now," Foley yells from within the hall.

Everyone moves at once. The villagers have all made it in, except Laynori. Why isn't she in yet?

She rushes for the doorway. Jorrin and Tavo move toward Felix, the rest toward the hall. Felix moans. I forgot about Jorrin's shoulder. He tries to pick up Felix with the other arm, but his face is screwed up. Together, they pick up Felix. While they struggle to get him moving, the darkness lunges toward them. I thrust my sword out toward where I think it's going to land. The boys ignore me, except to move faster.

The thing darts around me and heads for Laynori instead. She screams. Foley howls with rage. Whatever it is darts away. Foley scoops Laynori into his arms and runs inside. The boys

132

still have a few yards. I think they're going to make it when the dark creature scampers back out.

I thrust out my sword. The thing darts under it. I whip my sword down and to the side, catching its hind end. It makes an angry, repetitive sound. Did it just baa?

It darts away again. I follow it with my Zophasken as it sprints around us.

"Get in, get in!" Whatever that thing is, it's fast.

It plunges forward again, aiming for the boys. I move to block it, holding my torch out to catch another glimpse of it. If I know what I'm fighting, it will be easier to find a weakness. It moves to the right. I follow, but it jumps back to the left. I move with it.

It turns on me. Its red eyes glow above a long dark nose with a white streak down the side. It's the sheep that was staring at us when we first came to the village. Though this is like no sheep I've ever seen. It opens its mouth, making a strange baa-like growl, its sharp teeth dripping with saliva and what I think is Felix's blood.

I don't let my shock and disgust slow me. I jump for it, lunge my sword toward its neck. It slinks away, then bounces back, its teeth heading for my bad ankle. I thrust both my sword and torch at it. It backs away.

"We're in," Jorrin yells. "Leave it, Kaylyn."

I don't want to. I need to finish this. The sheep lunges toward me. I jump backward, swiping at it. It's faster than me. Its nose butts against my shin.

"Kaylyn, please. Laynori needs you," Marsa says.

Though I need to finish the fight, I let her words pull me back toward the door. I don't know if I could win anyway. This sheep is just too fast. As I back away, it vaults for me. I hack at it, connecting with its right shoulder, but it keeps coming like I didn't even hit it. From inside, someone throws a lit torch. It hits the sheep, which lets out an angry baa.

It gives me just enough time to scramble in the door. The beast springs for me. The animal hits the now closed door with a thud. Marsa presses herself against the door while Azleco lowers the beam. Or he tries to, but as he nears, the door lurches again. Jorrin slams himself against it next to Marsa, and I follow, throwing my whole weight into helping them.

There are two more thuds followed by silence. But I can still feel it. It's just sitting out there.

I can't do anything about it now.

Another thud, and the door groans in protest. Then nothing.

I'm not taking chances. "Pile whatever you can against the door."

No time is wasted following my orders. Soon, every spare item of furniture is stacked against the door. I move as they heap it up, only to stand nearby with my sword ready to slice anything that could break through. Marsa and Jorrin join me, ready to help cut the beast down. There's another thud. And another. And another, the door groaning, but not moving an inch next to all the furniture.

Then silence. Deadly silence.

"Add anything else that can be spared to that pile."

The villagers jump to obey, faces white and drawn. How much worse would their expressions be if they saw what I saw?

"What was that?" Sosha asks, yanking me from the morbid thoughts.

My hands are shaking, my fingers locked around my sword. "A sheep."

Silence follows.

Behind me, Azleco says, "A sheep did this?"

I whirl around to see Laynori lying limp in Foley's arms, both covered with her blood. Azleco is frantically trying to help. I rush over, but even before checking, I can tell it's too late. I sit down next to Foley and put my hand on his arm. He groans, pressing Laynori closer to him.

"She'll live. She has to." His mutterings turn to a howl. "She has to live!"

As some of her blood seeps onto me, so does the realization of my failure. Again.

Foley didn't really have any time with his new wife. If it weren't for me, they would have been together for months before this. Her blood wouldn't be marring the scene.

It's cold. So cold.

Chapter Thirteen

As others come to help Foley, to take care of Laynori and comfort him, I ease away. But I can't get far. People bump into me everywhere I turn. There's nowhere I can go that isn't filled with villagers. Sosha and Jorrin surround me, trying to give me some privacy.

Jorrin whispers that Granny is with Felix, and his wounds aren't nearly as bad as Laynori's. I should go to him. Help fix him up. But my feet feel as if they've been trapped in sludge.

"What are we going to do?" Sosha asks. "Are we going to be able to leave with that insane sheep trying to attack us? Is it going to maul more villagers if we try?"

I'm numb.

"So that's it, then?" Tavo says. "We're all dead. After working all our lives to rid the planet of Malryx, we're to die by starvation or sheep."

I should discourage such negative talk but can't bring myself to when I feel the same way. When it's all my fault. I couldn't save her.

"Keep your voice down." Jorrin glances at the mourning villagers. "Focusing on the bad won't help us come up with any solutions."

"He's right," Azleco says, joining us. He must have washed up; there's no more blood on him. "We've got to figure out a way out of here."

"We can fight off the sheep," Jorrin says.

"Were you not there?" Sosha snaps. "That thing is insane."

"I saw, but I know Kaylyn. She can get us past it."

If I couldn't save one girl from them, how does he expect me to save a whole village and all of them?

"How?" Marsa asks, mirroring my thoughts. "If Kaylyn couldn't defeat it before, how could she now? And what if there are more out there?"

The room grows colder.

Everyone looks to me. They shouldn't.

"I think we all need to step back from the problem," Jorrin says. "We'll take a few hours to rest up and think of ideas. It's worked before. We'll come up with an idea again."

"But what if we manage to make it out of here and back home only to find that this evil has taken over there as well?" Sosha asks.

As if the task didn't seem insurmountable enough already.

"We'll deal with that if it comes," Jorrin persists. "Get some rest, and use that time to think. We'll meet back up in an hour."

Everyone dumps their packs and stretches

out away from the villagers. Except Jorrin. He moves among the villagers, talking, offering a listening ear and a comforting hand. I should be helping him, but I slink off on my own. I pick the a dark and deserted corner farthest from anyone. I'm not fit for company, and it's harder to think with others around.

With my Zophasken, I still feel the sheep moving around the building. I focus on it, analyzing the way it moves and where it goes. I close my eyes and follow its movement with icy, burning stabs to my Zophasken. But it's no use. I'm learning nothing that can help. I'm about to pull my powers back, when I feel a second spot of evil shifting like the first. Marsa was right. There's more than one.

This is so much worse. Are they all going to be as heinous as that first sheep that attacked us? If so, we may as well stay in here and starve. Better that than being mauled to death by a sheep. I suppose some would prefer the quicker death, but I won't allow myself to be killed by something I should be able to outsmart and outmaneuver.

It should be easier now that we know the sheep are out there. Without the surprise attack, we should be able to strategize. But it was so fast. Even when fighting Malryx, their abilities were like our own. Whatever has changed this sheep seems to have changed more than just its dark wool and aggression level.

It wasn't like fighting a person, which

makes everything we trained for moot. Plus, we have a whole group of untrained villagers. How do we fight off the sheep and keep the people safe? We'll have to fight and kill the sheep before we can get the villagers out. But I don't know how many more are out there. There's at least three moving around, but I lose track of them as soon as they hold still, so it's hard to tell. They blend into the surrounding darkness. Plus, the pain of following them doesn't make it any easier.

That pen had to hold more than three sheep. The question is, how many were in the flock? And how many survived long enough to turn ravenous? Are there other animals out there that didn't escape before they were turned like these monsters? All these thoughts trouble me. I don't know how to handle this. How to fix anything.

I lie back and rest my head on my pack. We could all go out, stand at the door so we have something at our back, and wait for them to attack us. We'd be able to escape back inside if necessary, but then they could slip past and get to Felix. I don't want him in more danger. And what if they don't come to us? What if we have to go to them? In the dark, in the open, we won't have much of a chance.

The ladder to the roof catches my eye. I glance at the others. They're gathered together. Jorrin is lying down. Others are eating and talking quietly. Marsa looks as if she fell asleep. The villagers are quiet.

I gather my pack and climb up the wall to the hole. It may help give me some new ideas on how to get out of this situation. After checking to make sure nothing is on the roof, at least as far as I can see, which isn't far enough, I heave myself up. Without a torch, it's dark. So dark I can't see my hand in front of my face. I feel my way around. There are still a table and chairs out here from the wedding.

I find an empty spot and lie down and stare at the sky. Except there's no sky to stare at. It's like being in a cave. A deep, dark, narrow cave that presses in on me, even when I can't see the walls.

No new ideas. Without being able to see, it's hard to come up with anything. What did it look like on the night of the wedding? It's hard to remember. Vague impressions of houses dotting the village and the forest are all I can remember. The forest sticks out in my mind more than anything else.

I could come back later with a torch, but with the faint light they're putting off in the open like this, it wouldn't do much good anyway. Besides, I don't like the idea of letting the sheep see me up here. The sheep that attacked had intelligence in its eyes. I'm not sure it would really know what I'm doing, but a strong part of me doesn't want to chance it.

A faint shuffle sounds by the ladder. I sit up and silently pull out my sword. Even though my Zophasken has already recognized the twinkle of goodness, my hand seems to move of its own accord.

"Whoa, Kaylyn. It's just me," Jorrin whispers.

I force myself to sheathe my sword. "What are you doing up here?"

"Coming to ask you the same thing. Where are you?"

"There's a table to your right. I'm just past that on the ground. On the floor of the roof. Or whatever. I'm just over here."

Something bumps into my leg. His hand reaches down and touches my hair. "Found you."

Those two little words send sparks through me, warming the iciness inside. He sits next to me, his presence comforting. I wish I could see his face.

"What are you doing up here?" he asks.

"Thinking."

"And is that getting you anywhere?"

Sigh. "Not yet."

"Me neither."

After a few moments of silence, he says, "How's your leg?"

"Leg-like. How's your shoulder?"

"Shoulder-like."

"Are the bandages holding up?"

"Are yours?"

I stick my tongue out at him even though he can't see it. "Do you miss the way things were back when we were Zophas? Officially, I

142

mean."

"I missed it before I left. The less I did, the more useless I felt."

Despite the darkness, I nod.

"It had to be worse for you," he says. "The rest of us ran out of quests, but you were working hard right up until the end."

"Not hard enough. Showna still died."

"And what? You think you could have stopped that?" His hand brushes against my arm, and then he traces his fingers down its length until they wind around my own. "What were you doing before then? Before you found Showna like that?"

"Patrolling the other side of the mountain and taking time for myself."

"And why were you doing that?"

My chest tightens. "Because she asked me to."

"So you were doing exactly what you were supposed to."

"But she—"

"No, Kaylyn. You were doing what you were supposed to, and she was doing what she needed to. It's not your fault she died."

Maybe he's right, but even if he is, it doesn't change the fact that it still feels like my fault. "None of this is helping us figure out how to get away from the sheep."

"Maybe not," he says, "but it's nice being with you again."

The darkness is welcome for the first time

as my face heats. Though I've enjoyed being with him, far more than I probably should, given the circumstances, I can't help but worry about what Marsa would think or say if she knew we were here together, alone in the dark. It should be her with him and not me. I sigh and pull away from him.

"The sheep that attacked Laynori seemed smart."

He sighs. "And fast."

"Do you think they have changed more than just becoming crazed? Become more advanced like us?"

"It's possible. Why?"

"Are they smart enough to avoid walking into a trap?"

He chuckles, but there's an undercurrent to it I don't understand. "You haven't changed a bit. What are you thinking?"

"If we could figure out how to lure the sheep into the hall and close the door, we could escape off the roof."

"Not a bad idea, but how are we going to get them in, and how are we going to do it without ending up like Laynori?"

"With some help."

"Let's go get some help, then."

He stands, and his fingers brush my shoulder in the dark. "Let me assist you."

It feels strange putting my hand in his, letting him guide me to the ladder. When he lets go and holds the hatch open for me, my skin is

144

cold. I climb down. Marsa eyes us as we walk in together. I move away from Jorrin on the pretense of checking the villagers. Except it's not much of a pretense. I need to know if there's anyone who we'll have a difficult time lowering to the ground with a rope.

The villagers are melancholy. I don't tell them the plan yet. First the other Zophas need to hear it. But if they agree, we'll be getting everyone out of here soon. As I go, I finally bring myself to check on Felix. A villager is sitting with him, but I don't say anything since I don't want to disturb Felix, who is asleep. He's pale, much too pale for how minor his wounds are supposed to be. Did that sheep do something more than bite him? I carefully check over his bandages, but it looks as if Granny did a superb job fixing him up.

I finish my rounds with the villagers, trying not to let my thoughts linger too long on Felix. Once I've made an inventory of what I think we'll need to help get everyone down and out of this madness, I make my way over to where Jorrin has joined the others.

"Did you tell them?" I ask Jorrin.

"I was waiting for you."

"Let's get to it, then." I face the others. "Jorrin and I have an idea as to how we might get out. Did anyone else think of a plan?"

"Maybe," Marsa says. "At least it's the best I could come up with."

"What is it?" I ask.

145

"Simple. All of us go outside while we leave the villagers in here with the door closed. We stick together and fight off the sheep. When we've killed them all, we go. If we work together, I'm sure we can do it. Give a chance for at least some of the villagers to make it. It was hard last time because only Kaylyn was fighting them off."

"Can I just say, it feels ridiculous to be talking so seriously about attacking sheep," Tavo interjects.

So true. But the sheep are a problem, and the plan might work. It'd be easier than my plan anyway.

Azleco turns to Jorrin and me. "What was your plan?"

Jorrin nudges me.

"We had an idea that's a little different. We were thinking of having the villagers wait on the roof," I say. "We'll rig a way to open and close the door from up there. The rest of us will lure the sheep into the hall. When they're all inside, we'll have someone close the door and then get on the roof. The sheep will be trapped inside, whether or not we kill them. And if we're lucky, there will be few or no injuries."

Though it's probably a false hope.

With a hesitance stronger than usual, Marsa says, "It's a good plan, but there are a lot more moving parts with it. Parts that could go wrong."

"There is a potential for problems," Tavo

adds.

"And it's likely those of us being lures won't make it," Sosha joins in. "Not that I mind giving my life for them, but it is a fact. We're already down on numbers with Felix injured. The villagers are going to need at least two of us to get them to our home safely, I think."

"We won't need all of us in the hall," Jorrin says. "Just enough to trick the sheep into coming in."

I bite my lip so I don't join in with the protests. It is the best option, even if it feels like the wrong one.

"I can rig the door. It should help keep more people safe," Azleco says. "I think we should go for it."

"I don't like it," Sosha says. "But I agree. The sooner we get working on it, the sooner we can be out of here."

"Let's do it then," Jorrin says.

I'm not sure going with my plan is the best idea. Are they only voting for it because I'm supposed to be their leader now? What if I'm choosing wrong? What if I'm forcing all of us to go through what Felix is now suffering?

I glance at Marsa wanting her thoughts after all this discussion. She shrugs like she doesn't care, but her gaze focuses on the floor. Neither of us likes it, but it looks as if that's what we're doing.

Chapter Fourteen

It doesn't take Azleco long to rig the door to open and close from the roof. Only we don't dare test it, so we have to hope it works. It looks sound enough, and he's done this sort of thing before. He's always been good with fixing things.

He's waiting on the roof with Tavo, Sosha, and Felix. After a long deliberation, we decided the less of us down in the hall, the less people can get hurt. It doesn't take long to convince the villagers this is a good idea. They follow directions even better than before. Foley carrying the now clean and wrapped up body of his now dead wife to the roof had a strong impact on them. Hopefully, the plan will work well enough that we'll have time to send her to the stars before we leave.

Marsa is in the hall, ready to climb or come help, whichever way things end up going. Jorrin isn't far from her. I'm the closest to the door. We aren't sure I'm needed here, but I don't think the sheep will come in if we open the door with no bait. I'm sure we'll have to lure them in. And if there's any luring to be done, I'm going to be the one to do it. No matter how they all protest.

Jorrin and I each hold our swords and a torch to help get them in if needed, but Marsa holds only her sword. Tavo waits at the top of the hatch, ready to take things from us or lift us up. Hopefully he's not needed, but I'm sure he will be.

I signal to Marsa, who signals to Tavo. Azleco probably gets word from Tavo because in the next moment, the bar lifts from the door, and it swings open. Cold air ripples across my skin. My torch flickers and grows even fainter. If it gets any dimmer, we won't have any light.

Other than the darkening breeze, nothing happens. I glance back at the others. Jorrin's moved closer, blast his protective ways. I can no longer see Marsa, but Jorrin's face is taut. We wait, and still nothing. The sheep aren't going to take our bait. I'm going to have to go out there and lure them in. Of course.

I point at myself then out the door.

Jorrin moves closer, shaking his head. "Let me."

He won't be throwing himself on death's path if I can help it. I wave him away and dart outside. My heart thumps wildly, but my grip is steady on both my sword and torch. No matter what I'm feeling, I can't afford to lose either tool. I'm more nervous than when I met Morphrac in battle.

Still, there's nothing. Where are these sheep? It's been a while since I felt them move.

Did they leave? Or do they know we've set a trap for them? We tried to be quiet getting the villagers on the roof, but maybe we weren't quiet enough.

I take a few more steps into the open. Then I feel it. The dark slithering and darting to my right. A second moves in front of me. But they don't come any closer. I need all of them here now. If they don't come, the plan will be in vain. Of course, if I wait out here too long, they may trap me instead, which would ruin the plan even more. If they get me, I can't help the others.

I lower my sword, not so much that I can't attack right away but enough that it doesn't look as threatening. And my fears about the sheep being smarter are founded. The two that were already moving plus two more creep forward to the edge of my light. The only part of them I can see are their glowing eyes and a streak down the side of one of the sheep's nose. The one that attacked Felix.

Their eyes chill me. If the sheep have become crazy, are there other ways they've changed, too? The way they inch around me reminds me of when I felt out a Malryx. If they've changed enough to test my skills, have they changed enough that they won't fall for our trap? I pray to all those in the stars they will.

I slowly step back, their eyes fading away as my light comes with me. Never have I been so grateful for my Zophasken. They're close.

So, so close. But I can't see them. I can only feel them. There won't even be a second's warning should they decide to attack.

I skirt around, careful to keep myself between the sheep and the entrance to the hall as I continue backing toward it. They don't follow. They aren't going to fall for the trap. Unless I make the trap more enticing. When I'm finally at the frame, I bend my knees slightly, and lower my sword all the way.

It works. My Zophasken senses five blobs of evil creeping toward me. Five of those things. Instead of tapping down my fear like I'm used to, I let it out. Give up my carefully erected wall and let them feel it. But I don't let it control me. I dangle my fear before them but keep it close enough that I can bring it back under control when the moment comes.

They like the bait. Once the five of them surround the door, they dart forward.

I zip my fear back to me, tightening it as I run. The five of them give chase, coming inside the hall. There's no other movement outside. Thank the stars! I run toward the middle of the hall but still don't sense anything other than the ones following me.

"They're in," I yell, and then one knocks me to the ground.

I slam my torch into it as its razor teeth snap before my face. Suddenly Jorrin's trying to slice at the sheep on me. The sheep darts off, but a second lunges for Jorrin. I twist around,

151

cutting its face before it can get him. It cries baas and hangs back. But more are on us.

Suddenly, Marsa is there, helping Jorrin fight them off as I get to my feet. She yells out, "The door's not working."

Blast the sun!

"Move toward them as a group," I say. "It's our only chance against all of them."

Together, we hack our way to the door. Smart they may be, but not smart enough to realize we're stupid enough to trap them in here with us. Two of us could escape out the front door and let the third bar it from the inside, but there's no guarantee the sheep won't follow us. Even if they all stayed inside, the person who stayed behind could end up dead before they barred the door.

Tavo bursts into the fray.

We reach the door. While Jorrin and I struggle to fight off the sheep, Marsa slams the door shut and bars it. The sheep don't seem to know or care what we've done, and why should they? They have us. I don't know if we can make it all the way to the other side where the hole in the roof is. Five crazed sheep against four scared people. Of course they're not worried. But I am.

At least those on the roof should be able to escape without being attacked by them. How do I get Jorrin, Tavo, and Marsa up there safely with them?

No use pretending there's any other way.

I run screaming toward the sheep blocking the path to the ladder and swing my torch all around while holding my sword out straight. The sheep doesn't back away. Instead, it meets me halfway, sharp teeth dodging my sword. But not my torch. It screams a piercing sound of terror and backs away.

"Retreat now," I holler to Jorrin, Tavo, and Marsa.

Thankfully, they listen, making their way as a group toward the ladder in the opening I made. I dodge forward, shoving my torch into the side of another sheep trying to block our path. I miss, but it backs off enough for us to reach the ladder and Tavo to push Marsa up it.

As she climbs, she yells, "Don't you dare leave us, Kaylyn."

I'm already holding off the attacks. The sheep are raging now, realizing we're escaping. So many attack at once, I can't think, just react, blasting them with a Zophasken-powered fireball. It hits one of the sheep while instinct has me fighting off the others. Matted fur blurs with swords and torchlight. Jorrin is next to me, fighting, but somehow also managing to push me back toward the ladder until we bump against it.

"Get up there," he yells.

I slam the side of my sword against the face of a sheep and slice it into another while keeping a third at bay with my torch. "You first."

"Stars take you, woman!"

He pounds a sheep on the top of the head with the bottom of his torch and swings onto the ladder. The bloody sheep are everywhere then. Snarling. Shoving. Snapping.

My arms ache with trying to keep them at bay. At least the others all got to safety. They made it. They'll be fine whether or not I am. I back against the ladder, but with the constant battle of trying to keep the sheep's teeth from me, there's no way to maneuver up it. The closest one growls, its mouth breathing hot air on me. I punch it with the hand holding the torch. Another one immediately takes its place. And another and another.

In a desperate attempt to buy myself time, I throw my torch at them and jump up, flinging myself backward, hoping against hope I land somewhere higher on the ladder. And I do. One step up. Not what I wanted, but closer at least. It doesn't deter the sheep, though. They launch themselves at me. For a moment, all I know is rancid breath and sharp teeth dripping with saliva.

I throw another fireball at them, aware of my ever-weakening power. It misses, smashes against the floor and dies out. They're coming for me. Then I'm flying through the air, toward the darkened sky that seemed so far away only a moment ago.

Before I make it through the blessed hatch, one of the sheep snaps at me as Jorrin lifts me from the wall and up through the hole. It connects with my foot. For a moment, I'm being tugged between the two, wondering why my arms hurt more than my foot. I throw my sword at it like a dagger. With a tug, Jorrin frees me from the sheep at the same time it howls in pain. I shoot through the hole, crashing with Jorrin onto the roof.

I lie staring at the dark nothingness, angry bleats and one pained, endless howl coming from below.

Jorrin has no hesitation, his words harsh. "I need a light. Someone bring a light!"

His hands run down my legs as Sosha hurries over with a torch, Marsa right beside her.

"Where did it bite you? Where?" I've never heard his voice so frantic.

"I don't—it had my right foot," I splutter out.

Someone else appears at my side with another torch as Marsa takes the torch from Sosha and holds it closer to my foot. Jorrin rips off my boot, fingers frantically probing my sole.

Laughter escapes me, high pitched and crazed even to my own ears. "Cut it out."

He sits back, my foot still in his hand. "It didn't get you?"

"Got her boot good, though." Marsa holds my footwear up to the light. The entire bottom half is ripped to bits, the toes of it missing.

I shiver. Jorrin double checks my foot,

hands soft despite the calluses. "It didn't get you."

"Guess I'll have to thank the cobbler when we get back," I say. "I always thought she did a good job."

"How are you going to walk around now?" Sosha asks.

I shrug.

"She's still got two feet," Felix says. Though he's still pale, he's awake.

I shake my head and laugh, this time slightly less hysterical.

"You made it," Azleco says.

"We all did," Tavo adds.

A hushed conversation takes place among the others while I let myself melt into the roof's floor. The darkness overhead is too sinister to be of comfort, but behind it I know the stars shine, and it gives me hope. If I made it out of that alive and uninjured, anything is possible.

"You're smiling," Jorrin says, his own face still grim.

"Can't help it. I'm alive." My eyes feel embarrassingly wet, but I ignore them. "Thank you."

He leans closer.

"Before you go celebrating," Marsa says, drawing my attention, "let's get out of here."

"I'm in agreement there," I mumble. Thank goodness it wasn't my already injured foot. Now I just have to deal with two weaker footsteps. Which is probably worse. "Just as soon as I can stand."

"I'm so sorry about the door," Azleco says. "I don't know what went wrong with it. It should have worked."

"Don't worry about it. You didn't have a chance to test it. We knew that going in, and we all made it out safely," I say, forcing myself back into a sitting position. Marsa's right. We need to get out of here as soon as we can. "How are the villagers?"

"Scared."

Me too.

Though the painful howling from below has stopped, the other sheep continue their angry bleating from below. I shiver, the noise brings back some of my energy to help us get out of here. "Let's get everyone out of here, then."

Azleco nods. "I've got the rope rigged up. I'll double check it, and then we can be on our way. Marsa, could you help me?"

I've never known him to ask for help before, but she trails after him, giving Jorrin and me a backward glance. We seem to be bringing out that look in her eye more often than we should. While I lie back down and relax, I continue to ponder on that look. The others move to get things ready.

"I've almost got it," Jorrin says, his voice low but loud enough I hear him over the sheep. He slips the tattered shoe onto my foot and ties string around the whole thing. "It isn't the best solution, but hopefully enough to get you home."

My heart picks up speed again as his fingers work.

Once it's tied on, he looks at me. "Why don't you try it out?"

But I can't bring myself to move. I want to reach for him. Want his arms to wrap around me. If Marsa was here, I'm sure she'd be giving us that look again. It's only that I desperately feel in need of comfort after the week we've had. I've never needed it much before, but Marsa and Showna were always good to support me like family. So why is it this time I want Jorrin to be the one to soothe me?

"It's all ready," Marsa says, disrupting our gazing at each other. And I was right. That look is in her eye. "And this time, he tested it out."

Jorrin says, "Good."

I stand and pace through the small area. "It works great. Thank you, Jorrin." I clear the sudden tightness from my throat. "Let's go, then. If you don't have your packs, get them. Tavo, Sosha, Jorrin, and I will go first so we can help the villagers and guard them, in case there are any more sheep out there."

"Do you think there are?" Sosha asks.

"I haven't felt any, except for the ones trapped in the hall. We should be fine, but caution is still needed." I try to remember what I saw down there. It all happened so fast. I can't remember if any of them seemed familiar or not except the white-streaked one. "Azleco, Felix,

158

and Marsa, keep a close eye on the villagers up here. "

"Of course," Marsa says.

"After the villagers are down, Marsa and Felix, you come. Azleco, if there's enough light for you to jump down safely then, you can untie the rope so we keep it. If not, then we'll have to sacrifice it."

He nods.

"Let's go."

The light isn't bright enough that we can see the ground, but by my memory, it's close enough to jump. It'll be easier with the rope since we can't see, though, and since we have to set it up for Felix, we might as well use it.

One by one, Azleco lowers us to the ground. I go first, lighting my torch once I'm on the ground. There's nothing within sight, and my Zophasken picks up nothing other than the five sheep we managed to trap. I beg the stars that those are the only ones.

Tavo and Sosha join me, followed by Jorrin. The darkness presses in on us as the villagers are lowered one by one. Maybe night is falling. At least I hope night is falling, and it's not something worse.

Finally, Foley is the last villager lowered to the ground. He's barely conscious. He stumbles.

Jorrin steadies him. "You got it?"

"I do." Foley's reply is heavy. And then we're all more silent as Laynori's body is lowered. My chest tightens until it hurts as

Foley insists on taking care of her himself.

There isn't time to linger on such things, though, no matter how much I want to or how I even more desperately want to give Foley the time. I glance upward. Azleco's torch is faint, but I can see the rest. It's like looking through a fog. I shudder to think we're all surrounded by it.

Marsa moves forward when my Zophasken senses a sudden skimping of darkness. A sheep is loose. All the villagers are at risk. Marsa leaps down, her sword coming down behind me. Someone screams.

I whirl around to see Marsa grappling with a blur of black. The villagers move aside or are shoved away as I struggle to get to her fast enough. It's like every one of my muscles has gone dead, keeping me from her when she needs me most.

By the time I see her through the crowd, she's lunging at it but misses when the sheep leaps away faster than my eye can follow. As I shove the last, screaming villager out of the way, the sheep darts and jumps at Marsa. It slams her into the ground while its bulk presses into her.

I smash into it, shoving it off her with all my weight and, more importantly, my sword. It slices right through the middle of the beast. The sheep falls to the side as I push it over. Jorrin's already moving to make sure it's finished off.

Tavo kneels next to Marsa's prone form,

his sword drawn. "Did it get you?"

I run my hands along her backside, not finding any injuries, and then move to her front while still being cautious. I didn't see it bite her on the back, but I couldn't see her the entire time she was fighting it from the front. There's no blood I can see yet. I take her by the shoulders. "Did it bite you?"

"I'm fine. I'm fine. Fine, fine, fine." But her voice is pitched with hysteria.

As far as I can see, she's fine physically but not otherwise. She keeps slapping her body, scrubbing it down where she's already bruising from where the sheep was on her. I wrap my arms around her. "I'm sorry. I'm so, so sorry."

I can't help it anymore. I burst into tears. The flood of emotions, held back until now, spurts from me. The crazed sheep almost got Marsa. She almost died because I didn't get all of them trapped in the hall. Because I didn't feel it coming after us sooner.

I can't keep letting this happen. All that's wrong has been because of what I've done. What I did. It's my fault. It always has been. And I know what I need to do. It should at least slow the progression of whatever is going on with nature. Once I help my friends get out of the village and have one of them sensing good with their Zophasken to lead them, maybe I should leave to try and fix this myself.

Chapter Fifteen

After we travel a ways from the village, where it feels safer, we stop. Laynori's funeral is quick and to the point. Almost indecently so. My gaze can't help but wander to Marsa and Felix, who are resting after their ordeals. It's hard to see them through the standing crowd while I sit on some logs a villager found for me. Of course they wouldn't let me stand. Said I was too pale or some other nonsense. I'd be a lot less pale if they just let me keep an eye on the injured and watch out for another attack. At least until I leave.

I try to pay attention and ignore my injuries. To give Laynori the respect she deserves and Foley the time to mourn he deserves. Or at least a start at it.

As the flames take her skyward, filtering through the evil we're surrounded by, I vow I won't stop trying to bring the Malryx back until the balance is restored. Until the evil that was our destruction becomes our salvation.

అ∽ఁ

Everyone is almost ready to leave, but

162

Foley is still hanging by Laynori's pyre, which is only red hot coals now. The last thing I want to do is disturb him, but we can't stay. The sooner we're out of here, the safer we'll all be. Even if it means disrupting a man's mourning.

I move to his side, words struggling to form themselves.

He has no such trouble. "Just leave me here."

"Is that what Laynori would have wanted? You to waste away after she was gone?"

He huffs. "No. But that doesn't make it much easier to deal with life."

I give his arm a quick squeeze. "We're leaving in five. I'd really like it if you would join us."

"I'll be there." Though he sounds anything but happy about it.

Five minutes later, everyone is ready to go again. Even Foley, though his expression is as somber as ever. Our tattered group clings together, the villagers in the middle of us Zophas. Before we leave, one of the villagers stares at the slain sheep and whispers, "Those sheep were my livelihood."

The haunted look on his face stays with me as I lead them with a torch and my sword in hand, readying for anything and hoping it doesn't come.

The air is still heavy and dark, but the torches have grown brighter the last few hours. And even more heartening to me, the evil is fading in the distance on the fringes of where my Zophasken can easily reach. Our surroundings are becoming a little more normal. It's hard to tell how close we are to home, but within the week, they should be there.

"What's that smell?" Sosha asks.

I thought the stench of rotting eggs was a leftover fear of the forest. It's growing stronger, though. "I don't know."

"It's the swamp." Foley speaks for the first time since we left.

"It didn't smell like that when we came through," Sosha says.

"Let's just hope the smell is the only thing that's changed about it." Not that I'm holding my breath with the way things have been going. Though maybe I should since the smell gets worse as we press on.

A few minutes later, my foot sinks into something slimy and cold. "Found the swamp."

"Joy," Sosha replies. "It smells like egg death."

"Ugh. Definitely the worst thing I ev—" Sharp pain stings my foot. I jerk it out of the water and scramble to take off the make-shift boot Jorrin made for me, all while trying not to cry out in pain.

"What is it?" Sosha demands.

Suddenly, Jorrin's at my side, helping me yank the boot off as I give a cringe of pain. Even in the dim torchlight, I can see my foot is turning red.

I suck in a cry of dismay while Jorrin's jaw tightens. He whips out his water skin and covers my foot in the liquid once thought foul but now a precious relief.

My head lolls back as I let out a sigh. "Better."

He doesn't stop, though. He thoroughly rinses the rest of the foul water off before pulling an extra shirt from his pack to dry it off. The soft touch does more to ease the pain than anything else. It's then I realize the entire group of villagers is watching us.

I reach for my make-shift shoe, but Jorrin beats me to it and starts cleaning it.

"I guess we're going to have to avoid stepping in the water," I tell the villagers.

Marsa lets out a small groan, which makes me realize she joined us at some point. I can't say I disagree with her. Just one more thing to add to the growing horrors of the week.

"I can find a way through on dry land," Foley says. "It'll take longer and will be narrow. It will probably go faster if we carry the children."

"So be it. Thanks, Foley. How long will it take to find it?"

"Normally? A few minutes. In this gloom?" He shrugs. "I'll try to find it as quickly as I can."

"Sosha, would you go with him, please?" I ask.

"Of course."

They set off together. While they're searching for the way, I ignore Jorrin's protests and walk around with only one shoe. A knife-like pain is screaming up my leg, but I get to work arranging the villagers. We determine the strongest men and women should carry the children and, when possible, give them someone to trade off with. I alternate them with the older people as well, hoping the latter will entertain the children and those carrying the children will keep an eye on the elders.

When we finish, my feet and legs ache, but pain is something I can push past. Still, Jorrin sits me down and helps me put the shoe back on. "It'll be damp. Hopefully, you don't get blisters. Better than nothing, though."

"Thanks for fixing it."

He gives my foot a gentle squeeze and goes to the back of the villagers to help stragglers, no doubt. Twenty minutes later, Sosha and Foley return, the path found. I send Sosha to the middle of the villagers to help, and I stay at the front with Foley leading the way.

It takes two days to get through the swamp. Two days of pain and a gagging stench the entire way. A few times, one of the villagers steps in the muck, and we have to stop to clean them up. At least now we know how painful the liquid is and clean it up faster. No serious injuries happen.

By the time we reach the other end of the swamp, the sky is darker again, and not a soul has enough energy left to be more than mildly grateful we've made it out. We quickly make camp for the night, and people fall asleep before they have a chance to eat. Once everyone's settled, I don't sleep despite my fatigue. I stand watch, hoping nothing attacks for fear I'm too weak to do anything about it.

·

Chapter Sixteen

Halfway through the night, Azleco insists on taking a shift and letting me sleep. Only sheer exhaustion lets me rest. My sleep is fitful and full of nightmares. When a faint murk of sunlight appears as morning, I've already been awake for some time.

The villagers are slow to get up and slower to get moving. I can't blame them after spending two days and a night in the swamp, but as time drags on, the already faint rays of the sun grows fainter. I light my torch to prove my point and go around hollering, "We're leaving in twenty minutes. Get ready, then help your neighbor."

That does the trick. They get a move on. Even Felix is moving quicker than he has the past few days, though still gingerly, and he's much too pale.

Twenty-five minutes later, we're heading toward the canyon we have to cross in order to get home. Darkness seems to grow as we move on. At first I worry it's the cloud still moving faster than us, but then I realize we're nearing the entrance to the canyon. How much longer am I going to have to lead them? When will they be able to make it without my help?

The day runs on, long but easier than the previous two in the swamp. We stop briefly for lunch and are off again. The villagers press on, showing a determination I didn't know they had. One I'm not sure I'd be able to maintain in their situation. But then, I wander around so much, it's hard to imagine what it's like to be so attached to one place.

An hour has passed since we should have stopped, but I keep pressing us on. My torchlight brightens a stone wall in front of us sooner than I expect.

"Finally something going our way," Tavo mutters.

Black and jagged, with cracks running through it and even darker lines streaking across it, this is not part of the rock wall we passed before. I swing my torch around, but the rock goes on both sides.

"We must be close to home," Sosha says.

We're farther than I thought we were, but is that good or bad? Both. Good for Felix, but bad for our village. What must the Aster and Astra be thinking as this evil darkness nears them?

"We're only a couple days from home," Marsa says, coming up to walk next to me. "How are you feeling?"

Like a complete failure. Of course, that's not what she's asking. "More energy every day at least. My injuries are healing nicely. How about you? You took a much harder beating than I did."

"I don't know about that."

"I just got thrown around by a tree. You got stomped on by a crazed sheep."

"We've both had a crazy time of it."

I snort. "That about sums it up."

Suddenly, there's a sound. Something that doesn't come from any of the villagers. "Did you hear that?" I stretch my Zophasken out as a reflex, running it across the area.

"Hear wha—"

A dark splotch, tiny but definite. "Did you feel that? Something dark is closing in from the left."

And getting closer by the moment. I don't wait for a response. I dart away from her, the names of the Zophas rolling off my tongue with a missed familiarity. The splotch of dark is zippy and moving toward us in a zagging fashion.

Within a minute, the entire village is gathered in a circle, with Zophas surrounding them. I stand at the very front of them, facing the direction the darkness is coming from, Jorrin next to me. The sword is perfectly molded to my grip. The familiar thrill of adrenaline racing through me.

Everything is silent. Everything except a strange humming noise. I bend my knees, ready to spring at whatever comes our way. Only, the darkness isn't coming toward us. It's making circles around our group as if it knows exactly where we are. The movement sends darts of fear through me. It knows where we are and how big our group is. I know nothing about it except it's dark, fast, and small.

I move across the circle, stalking it.

"Don't follow the noise," Marsa says. "Everyone face the outside of the circle."

I knew she was my best friend for a reason. Time for praise later. Now I keep wholly focused on the darkness as it continues its coiling path around us. I stop following it, keeping my feet firmly planted, knees bent, focusing everything on using my power to track it. Ready to dash it with my sword or flash a fireball at it.

It grows closer and closer, zagging more and more as it moves closer to us, sometimes high in the air, sometimes near the ground. Its jerking movements are difficult to follow with my power—so quick and dangerous.

Suddenly, Marsa jumps within the group of villagers, rushing for the middle. I watch her while keeping my powers and main focus on the darkness. She raises her sword above her. What is she doing? The threat is outside of us, not in the midst of the villagers. Someone is going to get hurt if she goes wildly swinging her blade.

But then the flick of darkness jerks toward the group and doesn't turn back like before. It dives straight for the middle of the group, flying over our defenses. Flying? It's a bird!

I chase after it as the villagers try to swat at

it with their knives and branches, but it's already moving again. The evil-consumed bird is darting in and out of the villagers faster than I can move. As soon as I try to follow it, it darts another way. If I try to preemptively block it, it flies straight. If I try to dash it with a fireball, I could hit a villager instead.

Marsa is having more luck swatting it off in the middle of the villagers. I rush to join her, but each step feels as if it's steeped in mud and despair.

"Scatter the children and elders amongst you," Marsa yells.

"Quickly!" And though they are doing so, it's like the same mud and despair have hindered them. The bird flashes to the weakest in the group, exactly between the big gap Marsa and I are trying to reach, like it knows we're the biggest threat.

Marsa lets out a battle cry, overpowering every other noise. Even as I run toward trouble, the ferocity with which she screams startles me. Until I realize who the bird is aiming for. Granny.

My mud-slathered, despair-riddled body becomes heavier than a lake of water as I try to make it. But I won't get there. Not in time. Not with how fast the bird is. And neither will Marsa.

As the bird dives toward Granny's face, Granny tries to knock it away with her makeshift club. Only the bird zips out of the way and darts for her face, attacking with ferocity of the rabid. Granny is howling in agony. Marsa's war cry grows louder, trying to drown out Granny's pain.

Marsa reaches the bird before I do and swiftly makes it no more. But not soon enough. I should have been helping her in the middle of the circle as soon as I saw her going there instead of doubting her. I stalk to the fallen bird and stomp on it, making certain it will never, ever again be able to do any harm.

I lift my foot and bend to check it, to make certain. My heart stops and unwillingly chugs back to a start. It's black. And small. And has a white patch between its eyes. Just like the bird Marsa insisted we save.

Chapter Seventeen

I shove the thought aside. Of course it's not the bird Marsa saved on the way here. It couldn't be. Could it? I glance again at that small patch of white, ignoring the red wetting the black wings. If it's not the same bird, it's a twin. Marsa will never forgive herself if she finds out.

I whirl away from the sight. "It's dead. Everyone is safe. Give us space."

The villagers immediately comply. It seems as if the mud and heaviness previously slowing me down are gone, making me move too fast. Only the despair isn't gone. It's stronger than ever.

Marsa is trying to get Granny to show her face so she can look at the injuries. To see what injuries are causing blood to ooze through the woman's fingers. I don't know why Marsa's so insistent, almost frenzied. I'm going to have to fix it. If it's even fixable.

"We need to see the damage so I can treat it," I softly tell Granny, trying to counter her and Marsa's hysterics. "Please let me look."

But the words don't have the desired effect. Fear of what's happened must be choking

Granny beyond reason.

Marsa is silently crying now as she attempts to comfort Granny. Tears aren't especially helpful at the moment, but they're better than screaming. When she speaks, though, her words are surprisingly calm and soothing.

"You can do this. I know you're strong. The other villagers aren't watching. It's just me and Kaylyn. We'll take good care of you."

The words finally seem to shake sense into Granny. Perhaps the older woman is prouder than I expected. Perhaps after years of assisting the villagers, the last thing she wants them to see is her unable to help.

With slow deliberation, she lowers her hands. Though Marsa's hands keep up their comforting circles, her head jerks away. Granny has no idea, though. She can't see Marsa or me. She never will again.

I've treated minor eye injuries before but nothing like eyes completely scratched out. My stomach churns despite all I've seen in my life and steeled it against. It's then I remember I don't even have my supplies with me. Sometime during the attack, I vaguely remember whipping my pack off so I could move faster.

I rip part of my shirt and press it to Granny's eyes to stop the flow of blood. Something for now at least. Before I can send Marsa after my pack, Jorrin shows up at my side with it.

"Need anything else?" he asks.

"Hold this." Once his hands replace mine on her temporary bandages, I pull out my healing kit from my pack and grab what I need. It takes longer than I'd like to clean and bandage the injuries. Once done, I'm fairly certain she'll survive if it doesn't get infected, but there's definitely no chance she'll ever have her sight back. I should probably say something, but I have a feeling she already knows.

"All done," I say to Granny and Marsa and then turn to Jorrin. "We should stay here for the night."

"The villagers are already setting up camp," Jorrin replies.

Thank the stars someone has more presence of mind than I do. The longer we're on this journey, the more I'm losing it.

"Let's find you a place to rest," Marsa tells Granny.

As they start off, Granny says, voice slightly marred with pain, "Don't you go fussing over me too much now."

I can't help but give a smile, albeit a small one, at her selflessness while I finish cleaning up my supplies. Once they're out of earshot, I tell Jorrin, "We're never going to make it home."

"Don't say that. Things are rough. Really rough. But we'll make it through."

"I don't know about that."

"Maybe so. But don't let anyone else hear that." He looks as if he's going to say something further, but Tavo joins us and Jorrin remains silent. Once my things are all cleaned up, I show them the bird.

"It's the one from before," Jorrin confirms.

"We can't let Marsa see it," Tavo says.

"Do we have a right to hide it from her?" At times like this, I wonder which option is the Malryx choice and which is the Zophas. I hurry on, not sure I want the answer to that. I'm not quite ready yet. "Tavo. will you talk with her about it? You can say what you think is best."

"Of course."

"Now will be the perfect time," Jorrin says. "Here she comes."

I step away from the scene to give Tavo and Marsa some alone time, but I squeeze her hand as I go. Jorrin joins me, and together we make the rounds through camp, checking that everything is okay.

The fact that I just left Tavo with Marsa instead of Jorrin bothers me, like a bur caught on my pants. This isn't the place to think too hard about it. Or the fact that Jorrin is still at my side as I reach Granny, who's peacefully sleeping, probably from some herbs Marsa gave her. He's at my side as I go to Felix, whose sleep is even softer than Granny's. His wound is a little red but less than when I checked it this morning.

Maybe he'll be fine. And Granny will survive, even if she can't see. The others can take care of them both. Home is just around the

177

corner. It doesn't matter if I'm ready to turn evil or not. Soon, I'll not be needed for anything good. Which means there's only one option left.

Chapter Eighteen

The next morning, moans of anguish wake me. I think it's going to be Granny's raw pain we're struggling with. It's not. Felix is fevered and delirious.

Sosha is frantically mopping his brow with a cloth.

"What happened?" I ask her.

"I don't know." Her voice is nearing hysterics. "He just keeps getting worse. I don't know what to do."

"Shh. It's all right." I accept the cloth from her hand and take her place. "Grab more water."

She hurries to obey, her lithe form retreating. I couldn't be more thankful she's gone. Keeping myself together is hard enough without someone else falling apart. "Felix? Can you hear me?"

"He's too far gone for that, child." Granny's voice is sober as she feels her way over from the mat next to his. "Been tending him off and on all night as best I can without sight. I'm afraid..."

Something too close to panic builds in my chest, taller than the canyon walls around us. Vaster than this light-forsaken cloud we're under. "Afraid of what, Granny? Tell me."

"It's too late for him. There's nothing anyone could have done."

"No. It can't be. Not him. Not Felix." My own voice is reaching the hysterics Sosha's had, but I can't seem to control it. Can't stop it. I lean over and wrap my arms around Felix's thrashing form. "Don't go. You can't leave us. We need you too much."

Granny's hand finds my shoulder and holds on, but it's not enough. Nothing is enough. I was supposed to stop this. Prevent anything further from happening to someone else, but it's one thing after another, after another.

It can't affect Felix. It just can't.

Granny's wrong. She has to be. She can't see; how can she possibly know how bad he really is?

A fever. An infection? There must be something more I can do. Some step we skipped. I rush to take off his bandage. Sure enough, the wound is swollen and red, yellow pus everywhere, seeping across him. It shouldn't be like this already. I just checked it last night, and it was a little red, but there were no hints that it was going to go so foul so fast. What's more, every inch of his wound is etched with black.

Even without her vision, Granny knows more about healing than I do.

"You're right." The words are choked, stumbling their way out. "He's not going to make it."

Granny doesn't say anything. Doesn't try and pull me from him or push me closer. She just moves closer to us both and wraps an arm around both me and Felix.

Sometime later, Sosha returns with a bucket of water, but as soon as she sees us, it drops to the ground. Heedless of the mud she just made, she kneels down at his feet, letting the muck cover the bottom half of her pants.

Jorrin followed her over and looks at the wound. "It's already infected?"

"He hasn't been like this long," Granny says. "Just sometime in the night."

Thoughts torrent through me. Words about it being unnatural. About mad sheep. About my making wrong choices. But there's too much emotion to come out in any way other than tears. Stinging tears that burn my soul.

Jorrin kneels at his side, and soon Marsa, Tavo, and Azleco are all there too. Without a word, we make a silent vigil over him. The villagers surround us, honoring our grief the same way we honored theirs.

Felix passes quickly and more quietly than someone who led such a life as he did has a right to. Marsa and Sosha sob. Tears run down my own face, but there's nothing—nothing at all —I can do now. No way to relieve the soaring ache gnawing inside me, ripping me to shreds.

I feel empty. As if a part of me has died with him. I don't know how long I sit like this, only that it doesn't feel nearly long enough but in reality is too much time. There are people that need protecting. No matter what just happened to my soul, I have to take care of them.

"Azleco, will you make the rounds with the villagers?" I ask. "Everyone else, would you prepare for the ceremony?"

"Felix just died. We're not being chased by Malryx. Can't we have a moment?" Sosha says.

"But more will die if we don't listen," Marsa says.

And everyone is gone, scurrying off to follow my orders. Getting ready for Felix's ceremony. A ceremony we don't have time for, but one no one has dared say a word against. I can't drag myself away to help, even after insisting Jorrin leave my side to help. To honor Felix the way he deserves. But I just can't move. Can't make my hand let go of his.

"Would Felix have wanted you to act like this?" Foley's words spike my conscious, but I don't look at him. Barely give thought to how long he's been standing behind me.

"No fair throwing my own words back at me."

"Would he?"

"Just let me be numb."

"You didn't allow me. I'm not about to let you."

I whip around, raging at him, all the built up anger at myself bursting forth. "If it wasn't for me, Felix wouldn't have died. I killed so many Malryx. I was the one who finished off the last evil. All this death and destruction is because of me."

"So you were the sheep that attacked Felix?"

I huff at him. "You know what I mean."

"Grieve for him, but don't let him stunt what you need to do." He walks off before I have time to retort.

It doesn't matter. Felix is still gone. But Foley's right. I can't let it stop me from doing what needs done. From preventing more casualties.

Someone else should be able to feel the village soon. And then... it will be time.

The thought is both lightening and darkening. I want to fix what I've done. To help my friends, the villagers, and everyone else whose lives I've ruined. But the thought of becoming the very thing I've vanquished, that I worked my entire life to destroy, is chilling. But it needs to happen. I'll leave. And then I will become a Malryx.

Evil.

Chapter Nineteen

After numbing myself as best I can to the torrent raging inside me, we rush through Felix's ceremony. The grief is too much to bear, and the longer I stay, the more I want to grieve instead of fix the problem. He stays in my thoughts no matter what I do, though. His laugh and smile. Even his clumsiness. Anything and everything that was his hovers near.

Our journey when the ceremony is over begins as fast as ever, which is much too slow. But it's getting us closer to somewhere I can leave everyone with a leader they deserve. Another couple days of hard walking, and we will finally make it out of the canyon. Never again do I want to have to step in here. Of course, if all goes according to plan, I'll be making my way back through here later tonight.

Granny's struggled to find her independence without her sight. Though she's doing surprisingly well with a walking stick, the tough woman is clearly wishing for her sight back.

"We should probably stop for the ni—erm, stop for a rest," I say to the others sometime after we leave the canyon. How long it's been night, I don't have a clue. If it even is night. The sky is inky and has been for far too long. Maybe night has come and gone.

Everyone stops and works on setting up camp, not bothering to hide their relief. Perhaps I'll get whoever is leading them next to not push them so hard. Then again, if we're too overrun by the darkness, I hate to think of what fate could befall them unless I correct it in a hurry.

Once the villagers are settled for the night, I gather the Zophas. "Can anyone else feel their way out of this darkness?"

Jorrin says, "I can. We should be able to make it out of here soon and then home. Unless you have another plan?"

His gaze reaches into me, like he can see all my secret plans.

"I sense it, too," Azleco says, gratefully cutting through Jorrin's gaze.

"So we all feel it," Marsa says. "How does this help?"

"It helps us know we're close," I say, thankful they can. No matter what I need to do, I won't leave them when they could possibly become stranded in the darkness. "I don't have to lead you anymore. I think someone else should take that place."

"But you're our leader," Azleco says.

"I have been, but it's time for a change." Long past time. What were the Aster and Astra ever thinking, choosing me?

"Are you sure that's what you want?"

Marsa asks.

What answer can I give that's truthful without revealing my plan? "I admit that it's definitely a change for all of us, but I think it's needed."

"Maybe," Sosha says.

"But that doesn't mean we have to like it," Jorrin practically growls.

"So who would like to lead? Or who do you think would be best?" Though I try to say the words with a positive spin, they leave an unexpected bitter taste in my mouth. A lifelong weight should be a relief to get rid of, shouldn't it?

"Jorrin," Azleco promptly says.

And everyone agrees, except Jorrin himself. "There's no way I can fill Kaylyn's place."

"Just the fact you don't think you can proves you're humble enough to deserve the position," Azleco says.

"Or just not stupid," Jorrin mumbles as he rubs his forehead. Well, more like he's rubbing so hard, he's trying to push all the skin off.

I lean over and keep my voice small, just for his ears. "I believe in you."

The attempt at skin removal stops, though the worry still clouds his eyes. "I'll give it my best."

"And your best will be good enough."

I only wish I'd be around to see it.

❧❦

It's strange to give over the job, to hear someone else giving orders, though I can tell Jorrin's just as uncomfortable with it as I was. His words don't come out with as much confidence as I'm used to hearing from him, but it's enough the others are certain to follow him.

When he starts making assignments for watches for the night, I volunteer for the first one. Thankfully, he accepts my offer. Doubtful he would, if he knew what I've planned. It sends an ache through me, knowing the plan isn't entirely honest. Is it the start of me turning Malryx? Dishonesty has always been a pet peeve of mine from the Malryx, and here I am practicing it. Guess I am well on my way, whether that ache means I'm turning or not.

"Do you want help?" Jorrin asks, once everyone else is settled.

Any other moment, I'd welcome his company. Especially after the time we spent together before. The time when we discovered how bad I made things. His presence made things at least a little easier. But I can't drag him into this. Not for any reason and especially because he's now in charge of getting them all to safety. "Thank you, but not tonight. I think things are getting better, enough so that I can spot danger by myself."

The faint smile on his face shatters. "Is there more to this you're not telling us?"

Before was just a bit of sneaking. Planning

something bad without telling. But this is outright lying. Even practicing with other Zophas to help us detect more with the Malryx was hard, and this is so much more than that. I shouldn't lie. But is a lie bad if I'm doing it for a good reason? I suppose even if it's bad, I'm trying to become evil, so I might as well give it a start. Only I open my mouth to say no, and it won't come out. I just can't bring myself to say it. Instead, I stay silent.

He shifts closer. "You can tell me anything you need to. I'll always help you."

Something warms within me. Despite the chill of the night, his presence seems to be more than enough to chase it away. Makes it even harder to do what I have planned. I bite my bottom lip. I want to let him help, but I can't drag him down with me. I won't do it. As much as I want to turn to him, to embrace him, I can't. Even if not for this situation, there's still my vow. Fighting all my desires, I turn away, scanning the area for trouble.

"Just remember, I'm here when you need me." He walks a few feet to his pack, pulls out a blanket, and settles in for the night. I have an aching desire to join him.

Instead, I continue scanning the area both with my eyes and with my Zophasken, but there's nothing. There hasn't been anything since we left the village except the canyon and the swamp. I don't know if it's some sort of lull, a trick by another creature gone bad like the sheep, or if there's really nothing out here.

The trees aren't as nerve wracking. They don't feel as bad, though still more evil than they should. They're less menacing, though. And without being so big and close together, they're less threatening. At least none of them have started moving yet.

Two hours later, everyone is asleep except for me. Even Foley seems to have given into exhaustion. The fire crackles, burning almost as bright as usual. Soon it will be time to wake Tavo for the next watch, if he doesn't wake on his own. He usually doesn't. If I'm to do this tonight, there won't be a better time for it. Time enough for me to get so far they won't come after me. I won't be able to help with them anymore after this.

I tiptoe toward Jorrin. His face is free from stress and cares. If I wasn't worried about waking him, I'd brush my fingers against his cheek. But there's already a chance I'm going to wake him, and I'm sure if that happens I won't get away tonight.

There's no waiting any longer. The darkness has been getting stronger. As much as I'd like to think it's the growing night, I know better. The evil poison of the air is like the weight of a mountain waiting above us to crush us all.

I gaze at Jorrin another moment before touching my hand to his. Despite the lightness of my touch, his fingers wrap around mine. My heart quickens, but he's not awake. He rolls onto his side toward me, his hand gripping mine even tighter.

My throat constricts, but I've already made my decisions. Things will be better for him after this. Maybe Marsa and he can find love once I take away their problems. The best I can do for my silent vow to her now.

His skin is against mine, just as I need it to be for this one moment only. I hope this works better than it did with the tree. He's a person, though, not a plant, so I have hope it will be more successful. Besides, I've taken what was offered from others before. I know I can give it all.

For a moment, everything in me tightens, my Zophasken knotting up close inside me. If I kept it, it would make me all the more powerful as a Malryx. Stronger to take down the evil infecting nature. But I can't keep it. Not when Jorrin could use it.

I whisper, "My powers are yours."

I gather my Zophasken tightly to my heart, and then let it flow down my arm, through me, to him. There's no resistance like there was with the tree; it gently ebbs away from me. It understands my cause. I give and give. All I can. Everything I have.

When I'm done, the world is darker around me, but my heart is light and my hand warm. This is the right thing to do. But I can't help risking one thing. I bend closer to him and brush

190

my lips against his forehead. The first time I've ever kissed anyone. It's not even a real kiss, but it's enough. My lips stay warm from his skin, even after I pull away.

I gently pull my hand from his. He reaches out for me, but I quietly move away. His face scrunches together, but he doesn't wake. If I were here later, I would tease him about not being a light enough sleeper. Poor Zophas' skills are rusty. He's going to have to change that soon enough.

I want to say goodbye to everyone, but I don't want this to be harder than it already is. Besides, time is running short. I can't even bring myself to look Marsa's way. My dearest friend for as long as I can remember. My heart is ripping into tiny pieces, torn to shreds by leaving those I love. By leaving my sister. But it's to save them and must be done.

As I walk away, I want to cry. This ache inside hurts, but I don't give into it. Instead, my lips remember Jorrin's warmth. I remember his hand on mine. And Marsa's ever-present faith in me and undying friendship. Memories to keep me sane when the loneliness of being the only evil person alive stabs at me.

Chapter Twenty

Though tired, I don't think sleep is an option. Neither is food. My eyes are gritty. I've waited much too long. Maybe if I hadn't hesitated, Felix would still be with us. Maybe the darkness would have had a chance to seep from his system.

Guess failing him takes me one step closer to being evil.

It must be daytime because it's grown lighter. Not bright as day but like shortly after sunset. I can see a little but no details. I'm grateful for the light, though. Without my Zophasken, I feel little of the world around me. Is this what Granny feels like now?

I head off in the direction of the canyon, but I have nothing to go on other than my regular senses. They aren't nearly enough. How do people live like this all the time? I'm so empty.

I keep walking, though I don't know where I'm going. As long as I'm alive and manage to become evil, it doesn't matter where I end up. But I don't know what to do. How does one become evil? Without so much Zophasken, it's hard to feel the evil, let alone embrace it.

Most evil acts I've encountered have been

things done to other people. Killing, stealing, rape, torture. I can't do any of those things out here alone in the dark. Even if there were other people around, I couldn't bring myself to do any of them. The thought of even trying makes my stomach churn. But then, what can I do? How does one become evil?

Finally, after hours on the move, I sit on a fallen log. There's a surrounding copse of trees, which is no surprise since we haven't left the forest quite yet. There's the sound of a small brook bubbling nearby. What can I do?

Maybe I'm trying to make this about something too big. Of course it's hard for me to think of a huge evil act when I've done very little evil.

I've got it! I can start with a cuss.

That's simple enough. I've never said one before, but the Malryx cussed all the time. Even some people who are not Malryx cuss when they get hurt or frustrated. It should be easy enough and a good first step. Right?

Thinking about talking aloud to myself makes me squirm.

"Sno-blot."

It stumbles out, more of a sad, disjointed word than a curse. I grit my teeth and try again.

"Snoblot."

Better. At least it's all one word, but it still sounds weak. I eye the forest around me, my cheeks growing warm at the thought of trying to curse to myself. It needs to be done, though.

What can I do to make it sound tougher?

"Snoblot, snoblot, snoblot."

Still sounds lifeless and weak. I can imagine Marsa laughing at my paltry efforts. The thought makes me giggle.

"Sno—" I laugh "—blot."

Giggling is bad when trying to swear. I clamp my mouth closed and count to ten. The giggly mood doesn't leave me. That's Marsa, making me lose focus, even when she's not around. It is sort of a silly word, though. Snoblot, like someone didn't know how to talk about blotting their snot. Where does a word like that even come from? And what person could have decided that it was supposed to be a bad word?

I let the last of my giggles fade away. This isn't helping. Malryx always sounded so angry when they swore at me. What makes me angry? Getting everyone into this situation in the first place. Just thinking about it makes my body tighten. This is not what I wanted to have happen. Not the result I wanted from all my hard work. I take all that emotion and throw it into the cuss.

"Snoblot!"

It sounds better. Much better. More like cussing should. But it doesn't feel right. It doesn't feel natural, and I don't feel like saying it again. What's the point?

This is wrong. Cursing doesn't make someone evil, and I can't even manage to do it right.

I made evil plans to get away. I lied. I swore. What else is evil that I can do without anyone around? I've pushed things so far, and I don't have my power. It shouldn't be this hard. Evil should be consuming me.

I glance at a nearby tree, small and still trying to prove its worth to the world. We were always taught to respect nature. Now the tree is a little darker than normal but not evil yet. Not dominated, like the living trees in the forest by Crowin. It should still be neutral. Still have a chance for life.

Even though I don't want wood for anything, I pull out my ax, hands shaking. Even as I raise it up, both hands firmly on the handle, it takes everything in me to bring the blade down without asking for its forgiveness.

Many chops latter, the tree lies on the forest floor, dying the slow death of being cut off from its source of life. I'm just staring at it.

And nothing happens. Nothing.

I slam my ax down into the tree, chipping bark. Again. And again. And again. Each swing growing heavier and harder, just like my heart. By the time my arms are too weak to move, the tree is a mutilated mess. Wood chips everywhere, deep gouges across the entire thing, with branches ripped off and thrust aside.

It's a sight that would leave Showna horrified. My insides feel even worse than the tree looks.

But it doesn't matter. Any of it. None of my efforts are any use. Even without my Zophasken, I can't become evil. No matter what I try, I can't. I've failed. An ache grips at my chest and pushes its way out with a sob. How many more people will die because I can't get the evil under control? How many more people will lose their homes? Their loved ones? How many more animals will turn evil? How many more of my friends will die? All because of me.

The thought of Felix passing to the stars makes me sob harder. What will I do if that becomes Marsa or Jorrin? There's nothing I can do to stop it. I've failed at becoming evil.

A hand touches my shoulder. I jump, my tears instantly drying as I'm whipping out my sword.

"Whoa! It's just me," Jorrin says.

I slump back onto the log, hand still gripping my sword. Of course he found me. Not only that, but he managed to do it when I'm making a fool of myself with all these tears.

"How did you find me?"

"Strange thing, that." He sits next to me. I didn't realize how cold I got or remember how warm he could make me. "I woke up to Tavo shaking me. Telling me you were gone. That he couldn't find you anywhere. And my Zophasken had suddenly multiplied beyond reason. You wouldn't know anything about that, would you?"

My cheeks heat.

196

"I thought so," he says. "With all the extra power, it was easy to feel your little bright spot in the midst of this forest. Never thought I'd be able to sneak up on you, though. That, I will never forget."

My bright spot, like a blemish that should be darkened, and I just can't make it so. But I'm not about to admit that to him. "It's cheating if you try sneaking up on a crying girl. You're lucky I didn't slice off your legs."

"Oh no, you are not taking this one away from me. There is no such rule, and you know it. I got you good."

"Fine. You win. Finally managed to get me," I say. "Bet you couldn't have done it if I hadn't given you all my Zophasken, though."

"You'd like to think that."

I chuckle, but the spot of energy doesn't last, and I have to resist the urge to lean into him.

"Why were you crying?" he asks.

I don't want to think about my tears. "What are you doing here? You're supposed to be with the others, getting them home so the Aster and Astra know what is going on."

"I couldn't let you wander around alone in the dark. The others are fine on their own. They can all feel the light now. I'm surprised you can't, actually. They aren't even that far away from us right now."

"Are you teasing me again?"

"No. You really didn't make it far into the

canyon." His face is grave. "Why did you leave us?"

I humpf. Fine. Might as well let my stupid plot be known. Maybe he'll have an idea I couldn't think of. "I was trying to become a Malryx, but I can't. I need to do it, but I can't, Jorrin." Tears gather in my eyes again.

He puts a hand on my back and moves it in circles. "Why were you trying? Why would you want to be something you've fought your whole life against?"

"How else am I going to save everyone?"

He cups my chin with his hands and makes me look straight at him. "You can't. You've already tried your whole life, but it doesn't work that way. You've tried so hard you won't let anything else in. Or anyone."

The accusation hurts, a sharp stinging hurt that feels all too true.

His voice softens. "We'll figure this out together. If I can't help, the Aster and Astra can when we get back home. You don't have to do it alone."

"But if I could become Malryx now, it would start making things better."

"You tried, didn't you?"

"Yes." The failure of my attempts still stings, hot and angry.

"And it didn't work."

My throat closes up. "No."

"And it didn't work because…?"

"I don't know. Maybe I need to give you

198

more of my Zophasken?"

His hands drop from my face but move to clasp both of mine. "It doesn't work like that."

"But Noresh. After I took too much from her, she became Malryx." My eyes burn. "I had to defeat her."

"That wasn't because of anything you did."

I pull away from him. "Don't try to make me feel better. I know what happened."

"But Kaylyn, you don't. It doesn't work like that. It was her choice. It's not possible to take enough good out of someone to turn them evil. They have to want it."

Could it really be? Did Noresh really turn because she wanted to and not because of what I did?

"Think about it," he says. "If giving and taking powers worked like that, why wouldn't we go around giving our Zophasken to the Malryx? Or why wouldn't they give their Malkine to us? Battles wouldn't be fought with swords and words, but with the push and pull of power."

"I don't know, Jorrin. I was there. I did it to her. She didn't have much, and I took it from her, and then she left to join Morphrac."

"She was thinking about leaving anyway. She had good in her, but that good was clouded by darkness and fear."

"How do you know?"

"She talked to me about it a few times. Not so specifically, but I could tell it was troubling her."

"This whole time I thought it was my fault. I thought I did something wrong."

He squeezes my hand. "No, Kaylyn. You did exactly what you were asked. You did what was right. She made her choice, and you made yours."

It makes me feel a little better, except... "What's the point of giving and taking Zophasken, then? If we are who we are by our motivations, why does the power matter?"

"You've had it. Now you don't. Can't you feel a difference?"

Like night and day. "I can't feel much around me. Doubt I could make a wisp of a fireball."

"Exactly. It helps you feel the good and evil around you. It enhances what's already inside of us." He grows more serious. "That's why the Aster and Astra chose you. They know what is inside your heart. They knew you would benefit the most from the extra Zophasken. They knew you would be able to do the most good."

And look where that got us. Though I did do it at the request of others, and it seemed like the right thing to do at the time. And why didn't they pick Jorrin? Is there something inside of him I've missed? All I see and feel from him is good. Much more than I myself possess. Is my friendship with him blinding me to what's there?

It doesn't matter. It won't fix the problem at

hand. "What if I don't want to be good anymore? I want to be evil."

"And why is that?"

"To stop the evil spreading through nature. I don't think it will stop completely with just me, but it started growing before I killed Morphrac. If I become evil, it would slow it down. Maybe if I can become evil enough, it might even stop it completely."

A smile tugs at his lips. "And that is why you can't become Malryx. Even your desire to become so is motivated by good. You could never be evil."

My breathing quickens. I lean closer to him before I catch myself. What am I doing? I can't act out on these feelings. Marsa has loved him for too long for me to try and stake any claim on him.

I jump to my feet and clear my throat. "Do you think the idea would work, though? If we found a way to bring the Malryx back, do you think it would stop or maybe even reverse the destructive nature?"

Instead of answering, he stalks away from me and bends down to inspect the damage I did to the tree. Shame and regret race through me, mixing in an unfamiliar wave of pain, burning and sour.

"If our theory about why things have changed is correct," Jorrin finally says, "and I haven't found any reason to suspect otherwise, I think it would work."

"If I can't turn evil, who can? And can we help someone else become so?"

"I don't know. If we want things to be better, we may have to."

A frustrated laugh escapes me. "Did you ever think we'd want the Malryx back?"

"Never." After a few minutes of silence, Jorrin says, "I'll give it a try."

"Give what a try?"

"Becoming a Malryx."

"But wouldn't your motives be the same as mine? That right there would make whatever we try unsuccessful. Wouldn't it?"

"Probably. But there are things that I wonder about sometimes." His voice grows faint.
"Things I think could possibly make my motives change."

Is he hiding things from me? When he says nothing further, I say, "What is it?"

He turns his back to me, words flying from him like harsh, angry arrows. "Why don't you return my feelings? Whenever I try to get closer, you start to respond but always stop yourself. Every star-cursed time. Why?"

I clench up. What does this have to do with him trying to become evil? I don't know, but I can't tell him about Marsa. That would break her confidence. Except, he deserves an answer. "I honestly don't know what to say."

"Are you playing with me?"

"What? No! Of course not. I would never

do that to you."

He whirls on me, faced etched with anger. "Then why don't you let yourself give into what I know you're feeling?"

Because my best friend loved you first, and I vowed to let her. And why do I feel like I'm being torn in two by a serrated sword? "There are others in my life who need my loyalty."

His brows arch. "Another boy?"

"Not that." Definitely not that.

He stares at me as if he's pulling the answer out from within me. "It's Marsa, isn't it?"

I gasp and back away. He grabs my arm and pulls me back toward him, leaving us panting only inches apart. "I love you, Kaylyn. Not her. You."

He lets go of me and storms off into the darkness. I gape after him, wondering when the pieces of me are going to fall to the ground and crumble into nothing like it feels they should. In protecting Marsa, trying to be her friend, I've torn him apart. My own insides feel like they're being dragged from me.

A long, *long* while later, he returns. "Come on. We've got to get back to the others."

He storms away again, only this time, I follow him, wondering why I ever started this sun-cursed journey.

Chapter Twenty-One

The forest is darker than it was when I first left. Jorrin's torch is fainter. Either the day is over, or the darkness is still growing. Perhaps both. We trudge in darkness for a while.

"The rest are still a ways away since they've been walking all day and we haven't," he says. "We may have to stop for the night before we reach them."

"We can keep going. It's not like there's daylight to make a difference."

"You keep grabbing onto me because you're stumbling. You only stumble when you're tired."

I grump at the assessment of my weakness. But it's true. Has he always been this in tune with me? "I can press on a little longer."

"Unless you trip and twist your ankle. Then we'll be even farther behind."

"What, you don't trust yourself to catch me?"

He faces me for the first time since we set out. "I will always catch you, Kaylyn. But I can't if you won't let me." He turns away from me. "This looks like as good a place as any."

I suck in a breath that stings my lungs.

By the time he's got a fire going and is heating what will have to pass for dinner, I realize I haven't moved. The rest of the night, I tread on in the same sort of daze. We're silent through it all. Even when I pull out blankets and lie down to sleep, we don't exchange a single word.

When he lets his feelings out, he doesn't hold back.

It's dark when I wake, but then, it's always dark. Though I know it hasn't been more than five hours, my body isn't complaining so hard. Once this is all over, I'll collapse in exhaustion for a week, but until then, I'll manage just fine. I climb out of my blankets, pack them up, and risk speaking to the feelings ogre. "Let me watch while you get some sleep."

"Don't need it. I haven't been up for two days like you have." His words are still gruff but not in the ripping-my-soul-out sort of way.

"We both know you'll do better if you get some rest. I've had some. It's your turn now."

He glares at me like it's my fault I'm right. I guess it kind of is. Well, no "kind of" about it.

"Fine," he says. "But if you're going to watch, you need your Zophasken back. Without it you won't be able to protect us from anything."

"You don't have to give it back. I'll be fine."

"Either you take it back or you don't get to take watch."

I want to bring it to a duel, winner gets what they want. There's not time for such fun, though. Besides, he'd have to give at least half the Zophasken back for it to be a fair fight. "Fine. But instead of giving it all to me, we should split it. That way we can both help, and we won't have to have this argument every time."

"Fair enough."

He reaches his hand toward mine. I'm so conflicted. I want to take it, but it's betraying Marsa. Even if he's not in love with her, it doesn't seem fair for me to be with him, to touch him, without her saying she's fine with it.

"Did you change your mind?" he asks, his voice flat, eyes dark.

"No." I slam my hand into his.

His fingers curl around mine, soft and gentle yet calloused. I can't help but grip him tighter. Why didn't I realize I had these feelings sooner? Why did I push them off because of Marsa? I've got to talk to her about him. Fix this entire situation somehow. It seems as impossible as fixing the tainted world.

"My powers are yours," he says.

Unlike the first time he gave me his powers, and the second time when I gave him mine, this time there's no rush. No Malryx coming to kill my loved ones. No hurrying to get away from my friends. Just us sharing power.

I let it move into me, calm and sure. Peaceful and comforting. Already the world seems lighter. We lean toward each other, the draw of the power pulling us together. Or maybe the power has nothing to do with it at all.

I'm open to him in a way I've never let myself be before, not even when others have shared their power with me. As we lean closer until we're just a few inches apart, the Zophasken doesn't just flow to me anymore but dances between us. It flows and swirls between us. My breathing quickens as his lips near mine. And I want them. I've never wanted anything in my life more than I want them pressed against mine.

Except there is something I want more. Something that makes me pull back and say, "Wait."

He doesn't look surprised. Only sad. The Zophasken hangs between us, still joined by our hands but no longer flowing back and forth in a dizzying dance.

He lets go, the connection between us snapping. He grabs his pack, lies down, and uses it for a pillow.

I should let it go, but I can't bring myself to. My feelings have grown too strong for me to push them aside any longer. I sit next to him, but I'm careful not to touch. It was so strong before. If we touch again, I'm not sure I can bring myself to stop his kiss.

"Jorrin?"

His silence says a lot.

"I didn't mean to push you away. That's not

what I want."

He sits up, fixing a look at me that fills me with guilt. "It's never about what you want, Kaylyn. It's always about what someone else wants. You're so good. So self-sacrificing. It's good to help others. To serve and care. But you can't let it become so great that it clouds out your feelings."

I lick my lips. The thought sounds almost dark. Not quite evil but more selfish than is good and proper. Yet I want to do what he says and let go. Want it more than I want to think about where his words are coming from. "You're right."

This time he does look surprised, but the surprise quickly turns to disbelief. "You're doing it again, only this time you're trying to give me what I want instead."

I resist the urge to lean closer to him. There will be time enough for that later. "No, Jorrin. You are right. I've pushed myself so hard to be good, that I've lost sight of what I want when I can have both. I want—" I press my fingers so hard into the hilt of my sword, my knuckles ache. "That is to say, I like you."

His gaze lightens, and he reaches for my hand. I give him a quick squeeze before letting go and putting some space between us.

"If that's true, why are you backing away from me?"

"I want to see if a relationship between us may go somewhere, but I would feel better if I talked to Marsa about it before we try to be more than friends."

His face darkens. "And let her talk you out of it? Let her convince you she's the one for me, even if I don't feel that way?"

"She never convinced me to do so in the first place. I only pushed my feelings for you aside because I knew she liked you. But if I talk to her about it now, it won't be to ask permission. It will be to make sure she understands where I'm coming from. To let her know I'm still her friend, even if you and I become more." I hold my breath, worried about what his reaction will be.

The dark look has left his face, but he doesn't look happy either.

"What if she doesn't like the idea?"

I shrug. "We've disagreed before and always worked it out. She's sweet. I'm sure it will hurt her, but she'll understand." Hopefully.

"I can appreciate that." He gazes at me so intensely, I think I might burst into flames. "But the first moment we have after you've told her, we're sharing that kiss."

Heat rushes through me, leaving me incapable of doing anything except nod.

He lies back down, and I scan the area around us for trouble, but the thought of our impending kiss leaves me wanting to rush to that not-so-distant spot of goodness and tell Marsa all about my feelings for Jorrin.

Chapter Twenty-Two

It's not time to wake Jorrin yet, but it's been getting darker, and the light from the villagers has become shadowed. As much as Jorrin needs his sleep, the urgency to get moving is too great.

I place my hand on his shoulder, but he doesn't wake. I enjoy the feel of his shoulder for a moment, the smooth slope of his muscles before gently shaking him. "Jorrin wake up. Something's wrong. We need to go."

His hand jumps to my wrist and encircles it. His eyes open but are fogged with sleep. When the fog clears from them, his grip loosens but doesn't let go. Instead he makes little circles across my skin.

The touch is new and unfamiliar, sending rivers of pleasure through me. I don't want to leave this moment, but the darkness is pressing in on me. We need to get out of here. Besides, I really should talk to Marsa first. He understands that.

"Something is wrong," I repeat.

His focus leaves me, and his face clouds with worry. "Let's go."

He pulls his torch from the ground, and

together we move through the growing darkness.

We rush as fast as we can. There's an urgency to every step, but with the dimness of our torches, it's difficult to walk, let alone run. Our Zophasken only let us feel the evil surrounding us, not the location of rocks and trees.

Though I stay aware of everything around us, I can't keep quiet. The only sound is us moving through the forest, and the silence of it all is dark. Unnerving.

Several hours later, we reach them, breathless with the strain of catching up. They're hurrying from the forest like we are but not as swiftly. Too many people, women, elderly, and children.

As we near, Tavo whirls on us, sword ready. "You found her." His stance relaxes.

"You're back." Azleco stops at the front of the villagers.

The rest of the group stops to look at us, and upon seeing us, shouts of joy exclaim from them.

"There isn't time to tarry," I say.

"Keep moving," Jorrin says. "We're not stopping again until we reach home."

They don't even wait for him to finish speaking before resuming their quickened pace. I drift around the edges of the group until I find Marsa. She gives me a short nod.

Now is not the time to speak with her

anyway. I can tell her about Jorrin and me when we're not running for our lives. And when there aren't so many listening ears.

Every part of me seems to ache from the abuse I've taken. Losing my cool and attacking that tree was a stupid move on top of all my injuries, minor that they are. The children are struggling to keep up with the quickened pace, and many of the others are helping carry them. I can barely lift my arms, let alone hold them.

Unable to carry the children, I don't know how to handle them. I try to encourage them, but they just give me funny looks.

Marsa helps them with an ease I'll never understand. When she joins me, I keep a careful watch on how she does it but still can't figure exactly what she's doing that connects with them so well. She puts the child that was on her back on the ground, and he scampers off.

"What happened?" she asks me.

I wondered how long it would take her to ask. We don't usually keep things from each other. There's been way too much of it lately. "I thought there was something that might help with the darkness, but it didn't."

"What did you try?"

How can I possibly tell her I was trying to do something that would part us forever? I can't. So I say nothing.

"Did something else happen? I'm getting this odd feeling from you. Like a strange mix of happy and sad."

That only makes me feel worse. I'll find a way to make everything up to her when this is over. "We should focus on getting the villagers home."

She nods, but her eyes are narrowed at me. I deserve more than just that scrutinizing look. At least she accepts not talking. For now.

Marsa makes her way back through the crowd, helping out along the way. It doesn't take long for Jorrin to be at my side. "It's going to be okay."

"She's my best friend. I don't want to hurt her."

We're still under the clouds when the village comes into view. My chest gives a painful squeeze. At least its light enough that we can see, but we need to fix the problem fast or there will be nothing left of it.

The sun is shining on the mountain above the village. Home is lit up like a beacon at the top.

"Tavo, Azleco, and Sosha, will you help the villagers get settled in the field for now?"

"Of course," Azleco says.

The three of them give directions to the villagers, but I don't stay around to listen. Marsa, Jorrin, and I hurry toward the village. Felix should be here helping as well. Probably making some joke to lighten things. The reminder of his loss is like a knife in the gut, but there isn't long to dwell on it. The village is in chaos. People scrambling all over with their

213

belongings and children.

The Aster and Astra must have sensed us coming, or someone told them, because they wait for us in the clearing by the mess hall. Their presence immediately sends a flow of calm through me. We've returned. Everything will be fine. They'll take care of what I could not.

"What have you learned?" the Sister asks.

Jorrin nods at me to tell them. "We think nature is changing because there are no more Malryx. Nature is trying to balance their loss."

Their faces grow shocked with knowing horror. They both stumble over to a nearby log and sit down. Mirgen, the poor woman in charge of the beastly cows, approaches. For the first time in my life, I see the Aster wave her away. "Not now," he chokes out. "We will speak with you all soon."

Her stunned face mirrors my own thoughts. Though I know I just delivered the most horrid of news, I never would have guessed it affected them so thoroughly.

"Balance," the Aster says. "Could it be?"

"All these years we thought..." the Astra trails off.

"What have we done? What madness have we pushed this world to?" the Aster asks.

The Astra straightens. "We did what we thought was best. We couldn't have known this would happen. We've never been able to rid the world of evil people before. Now we know we can't rid the world of evil at all."

The Aster's lips thin. "But the balance. We never even considered the balance needed for life."

Jorrin stays silent but moves closer to me. It's time. Time to bring up the most horrid of ideas, yet the only one I think may give us a chance.

"We think there might be a way to undo—" I wave my hand at the encroaching cloud, "that."

The Aster's voice is soft but with a strained urgency. "What is it, my child?"

Not letting my hesitancy show, I say, "We need to bring the Malryx back."

They're quiet for a moment as they exchange a look. I can't imagine what they must be thinking. I've had time to deal with this all. Not very well but dealt with in some way. But they have helped guide us here, though. Granted, I was the one to carry out their wishes. To fulfill the quest of so many, to rid the world of evil.

Finally, the Astra nods. "It stands to reason they need to be brought back. You have more experience with them than we do. What do you propose?"

I look at the ground. "I tried to become Malryx but failed."

"You did what?" Marsa's anger blasts through her words. "What would we do without you? What would I do without you?"

215

"You would survive, like you always do," I say, though I know it's not enough. If she'd done something like that without telling me, my soul would ache for months on end.

"Marsa, you know you're like a sister to me. No one means more to me, and I mean no one. That doesn't change the fact that I have to do what's right, what's needed, even if it makes things hard for us."

"By hard you mean impossible."

"Maybe so."

She flings her arms around me, and I instantly hug her back.

"I'm so relieved you didn't change," Marsa says, crying.

"Me too."

I'm reluctant to let her go, but there are things that need to be done. As we pull apart, Jorrin holds a handkerchief toward us. Though there are only two of us and one handkerchief. Before I can even remember if I still have mine or not, Marsa pulls out hers. I take Jorrin's, giving him a small smile. Once my tears are dried, I continue with what must be taken care of.

"As glad as I am," and I'm so, so glad, "it doesn't change the fact that we still need to fix this."

"Is there any way?" the Aster asks.

"We need to find someone to turn," I say.

"And we need to do it without telling them," Jorrin says. "If they know, it could

216

change their motives for trying to turn bad which will prevent them from being able to."

"And we need to do it quickly." I eye the clouds. Have they grown closer since we got here a few short minutes ago?

The Aster and Astra follow my gaze.

"Do either of you know anyone in the village who may be on the brink?" I ask. "Maybe questioning whether what we do is good?"

"I know of no one," the Astra says.

The Aster is quiet, gazing intently at the threat looming toward us. "None of the villagers would turn. I know of no one that would turn, except maybe the Zophas." He returns his gaze to us, crying worse than Marsa was only moments ago. "Being around evil so much has a way of letting it sneak into you, even if you think you're only fighting against it."

The words chill me. We're going to have to betray one of our own in order to save everyone else.

Jorrin's face falls, but it's clear he knows it's true just like I do. "If we turn our friends evil…"

"Will it make us evil?" I finish, the darkening sky churning overhead.

"We'll forever have guilt over it, whether it turns us evil or not," Marsa says.

The Astra says, "After all you three have done? You won't turn evil. If anything, you'd turn if you didn't try. If you gave into your own selfish desire to keep your friends no matter the cost."

Something about the word selfish almost sparks a thought, but it doesn't flame up enough for me to grab onto. Or maybe I don't want to.

The Aster says, "This is a choice you three alone will know how to handle best. If there is something you want, please let us know. What do we need to do?"

His turning to us for answers throws me almost as much as turning one of my friends to a Malryx.

"Gather the villagers. Both ours and the ones we brought with us," Jorrin says. "And evacuate them. We have no idea if our plan will work or how long it will take. They aren't safe here."

"How far do we take them?" the Astra asks.

"As far as you can," I say.

"We will," the Aster says.

"We're just sorry we can't do more," the Astra adds.

And it's left me feeling like a child lost in a giant forest. I thought they'd be able to do more. If they can't help now, they'll be even less likely to help with what's to come. We're more on our own then ever.

No matter how much they can help, they'll always deserve my respect for their efforts. I bow toward them, but the Astra puts a hand on my shoulder, gently guiding me back up. "No, my child. It is we who should be bowing to you.

Begging for your forgiveness on being so blinded by our desire to thwart evil, we lost sight of the need for balance."

"If we survive, there will be much for us to atone for," the Aster says.

And then they bow, giving us the full amount of respect usually reserved for them. It leaves a numbing sort of surprise in me as they hurry off toward Mirgen, who is waiting for them. I most certainly never ever want someone to do that to me again.

As soon as they are off, Marsa says, "We need to get on this."

Jorrin nods, looking as sick as I feel. "Who can we do it to, though?"

"One of the Zophas we left in the village or someone we took with us?"

I can tell by the look in his eyes, he dreads the choice as much as I do. We start naming people, voices so quiet we often have to repeat ourselves. Nothing is working, though. Everyone is too good. Striving too hard to do what's right and good.

A thought comes to me that makes me choke on nothing. Why him? He could be Marsa's other half, if she could see through her feelings for Jorrin. Why would I take that from her? Even as the thought wars within me, I can't help but wonder if he could be the one. I keep my voice small, respectful of how this might affect her. "What about Tavo? Do you think he could be turned?"

"No!" Marsa screams, face pale. She shakes her head, and when she speaks again, her voice is much more contained but still writhing in pain. "I mean, I'm just not sure about turning…" Her jaw clenches.

I should never have brought him up. As Jorrin thinks, he's silent, but I can already tell the idea is rooting within him too. "Maybe. He's good but sometimes troubled. He could be the answer."

I hope both that he's the answer and that he's not. "Has he ever said anything to either of you?"

"No, but sometimes he seems almost…" Marsa's response trails off, as if she doesn't really want to think what he could be like.

"Bitter?" I say.

"Yes," Jorrin says. "I think there may be a chance with him."

My stomach churns, twisting into a wave of guilt. Not only am I going to try and turn one of my friends evil, but I'm taking my best friend's chance at true love away. How can I not be considered evil?

Chapter Twenty-Three

"How are we going to do this?" Jorrin says, acting more the leader than I've ever been.

And what do I say to that? What can I say? It was one thing to try and turn myself. Even harder to let Jorrin try to change. But to make someone change without a choice? To force evilness upon them? There is nothing to say.

"If it's all right, I think I'd prefer to try and force the change at our old Zophas home," Marsa says. "We'll either succeed or have to try with one of the other Zophas. If none of it works, I think I'd prefer to face the end there."

"I would prefer that as well." Though it's even more like treachery to do something so horrid in such a special place. Still, there's no place I'd rather be right now. "Besides, if nature is trying to balance things out, it has to stop at some point. If the others leave now, hopefully they'll be able to stay ahead of the spread until they find a place that will remain unaffected by the taint."

"Maybe we should just leave the taint then," Marsa says.

After all my own doubts, it's harder to hear them coming from her. This is so the wrong

221

thing to do. But what other choice do we have?

"It could work," she adds.

"Or it could devour all life for hundreds of more miles," I say, desperately wishing there was another way. "Make it impossible for us to live. Who knows? Maybe it will become a fight of nature trying to balance out the mess we've created. It could result in all of humanity being destroyed."

Her nod is so hesitant, I doubt she's really fully behind this. But unless some miracle option comes to us, we are stuck on this course. Stars be with us all.

"I'll go tell the Astra and Aster so they can plan accordingly," Jorrin says.

Our gazes meet then, and I wonder if this will be the last time he'll see our leaders. If our plan fails, how long will Jorrin and I have together? He leaves much too soon, though not without a backward glance at me. Maybe I should have gone with him, but there's something I need to take care of first.

"Are you going to be all right? Helping us try and turn Tavo?"

"How can we change anyone? I know the consequences if we don't, but it's too horrid to even contemplate."

"I know, Marsa. I know." How did any of it come to this? And why did I so blindly follow orders instead of questioning things for myself? "I'm sorry I got us into this."

"You didn't get us into this."

I suppress a snort as she continues.

"It's been a goal my mother worked toward her entire life. That many people have worked on. The Astra and Aster didn't just support it but helped guide it along. It's not your fault."

"But I killed the last one. Nature didn't seem to explode with evil until I put it in motion."

"You were doing what you thought was best."

What everyone thought was best. Just like how what we're going to try and do to Tavo seems like the best option, but how can it really be? "Is what we're doing now what's best? What if it's wrong? What if we only make things worse?"

"I only know I think things will be even worse inside if we don't try to fix this."

"So maybe we shouldn't. Maybe we should stop trying. Maybe then I could turn evil and not have to force someone else. Just like the Astra suspects."

"I know you. Have known you our whole lives. Would you really be giving up, or would you be giving up so you would turn?"

"To turn, of course. Which would make me not turn. I just hate this." My words storm from me in heated passion. "Hate having to turn someone. This should never have to be. If anyone should go, it should be me."

"I know. I feel the same way."

Her meek response makes me grip her in

another hug. This is too tough on us all. I wish it were next week and we already knew how this all played out. Even if it meant we were all dead. At least the uncertainty would be gone.

Under the darkening skies, we join together. Anyone who wants to stay. Zophas, mostly, and Foley. I go to see them off, stopping to talk to the Astra.

"Please help them where we can't," I tell her. "My best wishes go with you all."

"We'll need them. Though I think you'll need them more."

I glance at Tavo, who's standing closer to Marsa. "I'm afraid we will."

Granny surprises me, though, insisting on joining us, so she won't be one more person slowing down the fleeing villagers. As much as I feel I should push the issue, she does have a point, and I'm most grateful to have her join us.

Once we help see the villagers off, we make the familiar trek up the mountain. How I love the burn in my legs, the aching stretch of climbing to my sanctuary. Even with what must come, with the nightmare I must make happen, there's a peace with going home.

Unfortunately, that peace is sucked away the moment we reach camp and Jorrin says, "Let's get a fire going so we can cook dinner."

The start of the worst night in existence. And I'm going to be the cause of it.

Chapter Twenty-Four

I stand a ways off, near enough to be part of the conversation, but not close enough to really be part of the group. With what I have planned, I don't deserve it. Only I don't know how to start it. Luckily, or maybe not so luckily, Jorrin has no such problem, the scorn in his voice almost visible.

"What a waste our lives have been. We should have been taking it easy instead of fighting the Malryx."

With that strategy, it's not going to just turn Tavo but anyone who questions our choices. Anyone who's close. I want to run the few steps over to him and slap my hand over his mouth. Instead, I stand firm, hand on my sword.

"Youth should be for playing, and instead, they made us waste it," Jorrin continues.

Granny grunts.

"What's your problem, old woman?" Jorrin asks.

I'm biting my lip so hard, I'm positive it's bleeding. Rude to a woman who deserves our respect. Is that what we've come to? Is it what he's coming to?

When Marsa jumps to her feet, I don't

know if I want to hug her or push her back down. "What is wrong with you? You can't treat her like that!"

Jorrin's shoulders tense, but the rest of him is cool and calm. He gazes at the sky as if he has all the time in the world. Or maybe it's just time for me to show him some backup, even if I'll hate myself forever for it. This just feels so wrong.

"Maybe," I say. "But it doesn't change the fact that we've wasted our lives. To think we could have been enjoying each other's company more if it weren't for all this mess." I catch Tavo's gaze and tilt my head toward Marsa, who's back to sitting on the edge of her log.

His gaze goes right where I want it to. Straight at Marsa with deep longing haunting his perusal. "It very well could be."

Just what we've been waiting for! What we've been goading him toward. An admission that what we've been doing is wrong. That he could have had the time with Marsa. If this doesn't do it, I don't know what will.

My Zophasken is already stretched out toward him, but now I put my all into gauging his reaction. Waiting and watching and praying to the stars that his bright light goes dark. But it doesn't. It twinkles on, faithful as ever, despite his doubts.

The other Zophas are discussing what we've said, but their lights are all staying bright, too. I slouch against a tree with a groan. They're never going to change. Even when pushed, when doubting what we've done. What our whole lives have been about. They are too good.

I move next to Jorrin, slump against the tree he's leaning against.

"We could try Sosha," I whisper.

"We could."

But we're running out of time, and I'm sure it would end like Tavo or anyone else in this group for that matter. None of us have evil intentions. "This isn't enough. We need something really big. Something life changing."

Something that's right next to me, but I don't want to taint. Something no one should ever taint.

He puts a hand on my shoulder. Here it comes. The darkness that's been hovering, the flaw that's been there all along, needs to be exploited. It has to be, no matter how it tears at my soul to do it. No matter that I didn't just promise myself I would save everyone all those years ago, but that I would save Marsa and Jorrin. It's a vow I partially have to break in order to make even a part of it true. In order to save even a few people, I have to break one I swore I never would.

I have to shove with all my might and not give just a little tap toward darkness like I've been doing. Still, the name comes out in the faintest of whispers. "Marsa."

Tears build in my eyes, and my chest cracks apart as I lean into Jorrin. I have to go to her and ruin both of our lives. Have to do it now, but I can't bring myself to leave Jorrin's comforting embrace.

"Isn't this a cozy picture?" Marsa's voice sounds behind us, making me start. I slowly turn toward her, each movement harder than the next. Hardest yet, seeing her eyes light with hurt and anger. "The darkness seems to be growing. The others would probably like you to say something."

She stalks away like a mountain lion about to find prey. It's not easy to follow her closer to the fire. I'd rather meet a real mountain lion, but we go anyway. And even though Jorrin didn't get a chance to answer me, I know he agrees, because his hand is entwined with mine, strong and warm and supportive, no matter what is to follow.

It's darker now, the sun completely covered by the strange clouds. Rain is pouring out over the valley before us in a harsh sheet of death. Granny will never survive this. No doubt many of us will die as well. We need to force Marsa to change now if there's to be any chance.

Lightning strikes, lighting up the skies with a strange purple hue. Another quickly follows, still the same strange color, but this one arcing from the other side of the valley not far from us. My skin zips with the power from the bolt.

It's hard to see in the darkness left behind. A strange calm settles over me as we huddle in what's left of our group. Many things have changed since that day a couple weeks ago, but our friendship is the one thing that remained unaltered. The one thing that never wavered or floundered. And I'm about to annihilate it.

"Maybe we should go," Tavo says.

"I'm tired of running." I pull Jorrin to a sitting position near the fire, the heat licking at my skin.

Jorrin seems to know exactly what it is I want as he scoots closer to me. I can feel the others watching us, bewildered by our sudden closeness to each other and our inaction to everything around us.

It's time. Can I really do this? I close my eyes and take a deep breath. This is the last thing I want to do, but it's the one thing I know will work. It's the one thing that will save people's lives. And the one thing that will hurt me the most. But in that hurt is a warm, flickering light.

I smile at Jorrin. A coy, unhindered smile. One I've never smiled before in my life, but it feels right. So, so right. I should have let him in a long time ago. Even though I didn't, I have to make Marsa think I did. The harder it hits, the farther she'll fall. And she'll have to fall far. Too far for me to go with.

The wrenching in my chest is sudden and cutting. I blink the tears away, hoping the sheen they leave looks like the glow of love and not the pain of loss. The pain is too sharp for me to take on the true glow of love.

I snuggle up to Jorrin, resting my head on his shoulder. His muscles are tense beneath me. I latch my arm around his, and they relax. He smiles down at me like I've given him the best gift. Like I am that gift. The warming within me is tempered by the harsh reality of what I'm doing.

I should have let him kiss me in the forest when we were alone. Now our first kiss will always be tainted with my cruelty to Marsa. With forever damaging the friendship of my closest friend.

Other gazes are on us. I can feel them. Know that they are boring into us, wondering what madness has claimed us. I only hope Marsa is paying extra close attention.

"What are you two doing?" Tavo asks. "We've got to get out of here."

I turn toward him, careful to keep my true intentions from showing, but I can see Marsa, hanging on everything we say. On everything we do. "I'm tired of running and fighting." I've shocked him so clearly, there's nothing he can say or do but stare at us. "You can leave if you want, but we're staying."

I focus my attention back on Jorrin. He looks at me with a peaceful expression, except for his eyes. His eyes are tight with trepidation over what we must do. What we are doing.

There should be something to say to him, but what does one say in such a situation as this? True words I can't speak for the ears listening around us and other more coy words the others should hear. I don't know. Maybe if I had spent more time flirting, I'd know what to say. Even though I don't, being this close to Jorrin is good. Comforting and soothing. It's already helping ease the sting of my current actions and how they'll hurt Marsa. It's so, so good. And yes, so bad. Dearest Marsa. I'll never forgive myself for this.

Despite the rancor the last thought brings, I climb onto Jorrin's lap, my back to the others. The first time I've put my back to a problem. It's clear what we're doing. Clear enough for the task at hand. Still, I don't feel quite as exposed with my back to them.

I wrap my arms around Jorrin's neck. He leans into me. He smells of wood and metal. I brush my nose against his. His arms encircle me, pulling me closer, bringing me to him. Our lips meet.

It's right. Good. We should have kissed a long time ago. Long before the end of the Malryx. His lips are urgent against mine. Urgent for me and urgent for our success. The kiss deepens, every ache and hope poured into it.

The joy of finally being with him bursts through me, shoving its way through the damage it's doing. Until the rest of the world fades. The heat of the fire on my back. The others hovering around. The rain and thunder from the storm. All of it drowns in the heat blooming where my lips touch Jorrin's.

Though Marsa is my dearest friend, I shouldn't have let her feelings for him stop me from following through with mine. Especially with his return of my feelings. I worried over being an unfaithful friend, but by keeping this from us all, I've been even more untrue. She knew he would never be more than friends with her. I knew it. I should have talked to her sooner. Not put her in this situation. She would have understood. Jorrin and I could have been happy, my friendship with Marsa still intact. So many things I should have done. But if I did them, the world would have never been the same again.

I wouldn't have any way to make her fall. No way to make her become what she needs to. My worst enemy.

Tears want to stream down my face as our lips move together, but I lock them in tight. I can't give into them and possibly ruin this one chance I have to make things right. Jorrin must sense my conflict, though. He pulls back and whispers, "I know. I've got you. We'll make it through this."

I press my lips together, pulling my hurt inside, until I can whisper back. "I love you. I'm sorry I waited until the problems of the world were on us to realize it. Sorry I didn't talk to my best friend about it sooner."

"What are you two little love birds whispering about?" Marsa's voice cuts into me, razor sharp. "Something you'd like to share with us? Something you'd like to tell your *friends*?"

My face crumples. A single tear leaks out.

Jorrin presses a kiss to my cheek and wipes away the tear. "You can do this. You're strong enough."

I take comfort from his words, pull them into me. No more tears. He's right. I can do what needs to be done. Light, happy love replaces my hurt. The sorrow is still there. It will always be there, but it's soothed by my doing the right thing. Without moving from Jorrin's lap, I turn toward the group. I face Marsa. "I suppose it's time to tell you. Jorrin and I are in love."

"That's wonderful," Azleco says. "Congratulations."

But I ignore his words. I ignore everything and everyone, except Marsa. Her face tightens with pain. It stabs at me. Her hurt is my hurt, even though I brought it on us both. But time passes, and nothing changes, except for the increased lightning strikes. Each flash showing Marsa's face not hardening but hiding her expressions.

I reach out with my Zophasken. She's not a bright star of goodness, but neither is she lost among the evil that surrounds us. It's not enough. I have to do more.

"We are to be married," I say. "Or rather, we will marry if we live through this. At least we'll be together in the end."

A flash of pain breaks through her facade,

but by the time the next lightning strikes, her pain is hidden again. Her flicker of light is faint but there. We've failed. I bury my face in Jorrin's neck. She's supposed to be hurt by us. She's supposed to fall. If she doesn't fall, we'll have to search the entire world for someone that will. We may never find anyone. More people are losing their homes. More people will die. I can't let that happen.

"You don't mind?" I yell over the growing noise of the storm.

The lightning grows in such frequency. There are more moments of the strange light than the blinding darkness.

Instead of responding, she shrugs. She's hurt and angry but not fallen. Close. So close. But my love for Jorrin isn't enough to make her fall.

A large part of me is relieved. I want to run over and hug her. Squeeze her close to me and never let her go. I don't want Marsa to turn evil. But I can't let my feelings for my best friend, the girl like a sister to me, the person who understands me better than any other, stand in the way of thousands of lives.

Suddenly she calls out, "You don't have to do this."

But I do. More than anything else. I've trained my whole life not to defeat evil but to save people. I will not fail.

I leave the safety of Jorrin, so she'll be able to hear me clearly. I move right next to her and say, "Oh, but I do. I've always wanted to be with him."

She stares at me, her faint light flickering. "I saw you that night you left us all alone in the forest. You kissed him, the man I love, before you left, but you didn't even look my way."

Only because I knew I couldn't leave you. Because I cared about him, but you are my family. "He was the one I didn't want to leave."

She turns away from me, toward the lightning-filled sky. "I saw the way he looked at you. What he said about not loving me was the truth. But I didn't know how you felt. I kept waiting for you to talk to me about it. For you to come to me."

I've never been good at lying to stop evil, but now more than ever, I need to make it work. I need to lie, to create evil. Please make that tiny spark go out. Charge her desires to be evil toward me, the sister who deserves it. "I did tell your mom all about it. It was easy to talk to her, and she agreed with me. She thought I'd be better for him anyway."

More of her light crumples, but still it refuses to go out. I want to crumple along with her, to fade into the nothingness, but instead I press on. That last flicker of goodness must go out.

"In fact, that's what I was doing that day when I should have been out helping her defeat Morphrac. I was daydreaming about how Jorrin and I would be able to be together soon. I knew my time fighting was almost over, and there would be nothing left to stop us. Guess I should have been helping your mother instead."

Her light is such a faint flame, I want to breathe it back to life. Instead, the lightning strikes become so rapid, they blend into each other, filling the air with their strange purple glow as I deal the final blow.

"Even with her dying breath, Showna wanted to help me, though I failed her by my daydreaming." I give her a cold smile. "Still, she always did love me best."

The small flicker of good snaps out, evil flaming from her. My heart shatters. It worked.

"You don't know what you've done." A flash of lightning casts an eerie glow over her.

Unfortunately, I know all too well what I've done to save the world. And I'll never forgive myself for what it cost.

"Your mooning over a boy caused Showna to die?" Tavo's goodness flashes out, evil bursting from him just as strong as Marsa's.

Sosha quickly follows. I didn't expect so many of them to fall. I didn't want any of them to fall. I want to cry, beg for their forgiveness, and bring them back. Instead, I shrug like Showna's death meant nothing to me. Like I was being silly instead of doing what she asked. For I know in my heart, I was doing what I was supposed to. But that lie told with the best intentions seems to be the thing that has them all turning. I have to keep it. Have to watch them not just flicker out but want to hate me for the rest of their lives. I give them a stupid grin and shrug.

"I will never forgive you, Kaylyn. Never," Marsa says.

The darkness surging from her eats at me, searing me with what I've done.

But the storm is calming. Already the rain is easing, more seconds between strikes of lightning.

Marsa screams. It continues, filled with hurt and longing, echoing through the air around us. No lightning strikes. It's dark and heavy with pain. Pain she never really released at her mother's death. Pain made worse by my lie. The sound makes me ache. But more than that, it does something even stranger.

As she screams, the darkness lightens, the blackness flowing to her. The sky that was blacker than the blackest night slowly starts to brighten. The clouds pull back, slowly exposing the setting sun. It looks like dawn, the sun rising, but going the wrong way just like everything else. And the sun is still reaching for the horizon. The rain lets up but doesn't stop. A flash of the purple lightning jets across the sky and in front of the sun.

And the darkness goes not just to her but to Sosha and Tavo as well. The sun struggles to shine past the clouds and the newly fallen struggle to control their anger.

"I will never forgive you, Kaylyn. Never."

Marsa grabs her pack, sword clenched in her free hand so tightly, it's like she's ready to strike me down now. Though it'd be exactly what I deserve. "You won't see vengeance coming until it's blasted you apart."

But instead of attacking, she whips away, Sosha and Tavo running after her.

And though my heart is breaking to see her go, though I want nothing more than to tell her the truth and bring her back, the world is coming back to life where she and the others walk. The world is coming back to itself. The darkness, storm, and lightning remain but are dying off.

A rainbow stretches off in the distance, spanning across the whole sky. Bright, vivid colors light from the almost ready to set sun. A second, fainter one spans the sky across it. A final strike of the strange lightning mars the sight.

Jorrin puts an arm around me. Azleco is close beside us, trusting, but still waiting for answers.

"You did what you had to," Granny says. "Would that it hadn't need be so."

And down below, already scampering across the village, Marsa leads Tavo and Sosha toward the diminishing darkness. I watch her flee into it.

It swoops after her, somehow lightening as she passes by, like she's healing the world. Except she's Malryx now. There's no healing going on. Instead, my closest friend and dearest sister is ever darkening.

Chapter Twenty-Five

To think I was once foolish enough to cry over never having an opponent again. I'd rather never again have an opponent than to turn my best friend, my sister, into one. In the months that follow, the thought haunts me. The world is slowly healing. Much work needs to be done to fix everything that was ruined in the storm and the animals that chased off in the darkness. We've not encountered any other evil animals, and the water seems drinkable again.

Back by Foley's, the darkness still lingers. It took a long time to kill all the Malryx. I guess now it will take a long time to bring them back.

There's been no sign of Marsa, Tavo, or Sosha, except for a few raids on villages. No one sees anything, but food and wares are reported missing. Sometimes a person or two will turn up missing as well. People their friends say were questioning the way things were and are. What we've done. Every time it happens, a little more darkness pulls away from the village.

I think of her often, but she's beyond reach.

Jorrin cups my cheek with his hand. "Are you thinking about her again?"

I nod.

He pulls me in close and wraps his arms around me. His embrace is like a blanket to my soul. I thought starting our relationship as a way to break Marsa would leave us damaged. Instead, it's made me realize it's critical to be honest about all my thoughts and feelings. Besides, it's easier to take on challenges with him at my side. I let him strengthen me, until I feel strong enough to handle the pain on my own. And I strengthen him as well, until together, we are ready to protect the world from evil. Just never to kill it off ever again.

I reach up and press my lips to his. He kisses me back, tenderly and gently, filling me with sweetness and light. Maybe someday the pain will fade enough that I'll barely notice it. Maybe.

"We should get going," I say.

He chuckles. "I'd rather stay here a while more."

I lean closer, like I'm going to give him what he wants. His eyes lighten, and I almost give in, but we have work to do. I dance away from him, twirling from his grasp with a laugh.

He groans. "I'll see you soon."

"Not soon enough."

I leave him, reaching out to him with my Zophasken. The link between us sustains me as I patrol this edge of the village, looking for any signs of trouble now that trouble is back. There's something satisfying about keeping people safe. It's what I was born to do.

An hour later, something evil brushes against my Zophasken. Before this all happened, I would have raced to it, ready to take on a fight. Now, I may have to fight a friend. But not to the death. No more Malryx deaths unless it can't be helped. The prison is almost done being built. It may be better than death, but I don't want to send any of my friends there either.

My desire to do good, to help my villagers, is stronger than my worry over the confrontation. I race to the looming spot of evil, keeping the connection to Jorrin to help strengthen me. It's likely that he will notice soon and come to assist me.

My pulse is erratic as I come closer. The darkness slows. I follow suit, changing to a walk. Whoever it is isn't trying to get away; there's no need to rush. And my knees are shaking anyway. This strange rapid motion. I didn't know knees could do that.

When the darkness is just beyond a grove of trees, I stop. I don't know if I wish for a stranger or a friend. And if a friend, Tavo or Sosha? Or Marsa?

Whoever it is echoes my falter. We stand close to each other, both aware of the other's presence. If I were to call out, I'm sure he or she could hear me.

Whatever has become of one of my friends, I can face them. I owe them that at the very least. I start forward, but they stay still. I cross the little clearing and make my way around the tree. My hand is on my sword, but I don't draw it.

When the last branch clears from my sight, Marsa stands before me in the middle of a vast clearing. My footsteps falter. I want to choke out an apology, but instead I just stare at her. And she stares back.

How long we remain like this, I can't tell. I drink her in, committing her to my memory for when she is gone again. She hasn't changed much. Her hair is longer, eyes a little wiser, but otherwise she is still my Marsa.

"You could join us," she finally says.

I wish I could, but it requires more than just a desire to be with a sister. "You know I can't."

"I do know." She shifts her weight. "We're very happy."

The worry of the fate I sent her to, which has been eating inside me for months, lessens, though I doubt it will ever fully ease. "We're happy too." But would be happier if you were still here.

She leans forward like she somehow heard the thought and wishes it as well, but of course, it can no longer be. Her desires are evil. Mine are good. But somehow, someway, there's still a friendship linking us together.

"We'll always be sisters." The words slip out before I can stop them, but her darkness never wavers toward light.

"We will. Only I'm the smart one." She grins.

Jorrin must notice her next to me, for suddenly his light is moving toward us. He's coming from the side, quickly, but not so fast we don't have a few minutes.

I move closer to her, out away from the trees. Still she says and does nothing.

"Marsa."

No other words will come.

"Kaylyn."

My name doesn't sound as bitter as I expected. It sounds the same as before. I step closer. "Marsa, I—" Can't apologize. Can't risk you forgiving me and the world going back to trying to kill us all. "Things haven't been the same since you left."

"Not for us either."

"How are Tavo and Sosha?"

Her grip tightens on her sword. "They're fine. At least as much as they can be after being betrayed and forced out into a world that has nothing to offer them."

The apology almost tumbles out of me. I bite my lip.

Her hand drops from her sword, her shoulders slumping with released tension. "I know you are, Kaylyn, and I understand."

I gape at her.

"What? You think we grew up together all those years, and I couldn't figure out what you really meant?"

"But if you know…"

She shrugs. "I didn't when you betrayed

244

me, but after thinking about it, I knew it couldn't be any other way. You would never do something so cruel without cause."

I double check her power, though it's still clearly evil. "But you're still Malryx."

"It suits me better than I expected." She grins. "It's so much easier taking the things I want and causing trouble. I like seeing you all scatter, trying to fix things like angry ants. Besides, you wouldn't believe what I've learned."

From being evil? Doubtful. And yet... "What?"

"Zophas and Malryx are opposites, yes, and you may have light, but it's not good like you think. It's a savage, brutal light that forces others to follow under it or be killed."

She's become so confused. "No, we help people. We're kind. We've only killed those—"

"Whom the Aster and Astra sent you after. Those who opposed them. Those who I'm now like. And all I'm doing, Kaylyn, is trying to survive."

"No, it's not like that. You've hurt people." Why am I trying to talk her out of this? It's what she's supposed to be doing now. And from how things have been going, she's pretty good at it.

"Have I? Maybe. But only those who tried to not let me survive. Those who would get in the way of Sosha and Tavo's survival."

"But hurting them? That's not like you." She may still be Marsa, but she's already

245

changing. She's no longer the sister I knew.

"Maybe it wasn't before, but now that I've protected others for a while—"

"You'll protect them no matter the cost." Just like I protect those I love. And in a way worth fighting for, not like those gutless Malryx from before, who barely knew how to fight. "I've waited a long time for a worthy opponent."

"You may have trouble keeping up with me." But there's a twinkle to her eye.

"That's what you hope." As wrong as it should be to be happy about this, the bright, sunny feeling just keeps growing. If we have to be on different sides, I can't think of a better way to do it.

"Don't worry. I'll keep your little secret about your true intentions from Sosha and Tavo. They're still learning what I already know, and they're so much more effective when they have your betrayal to focus on."

"You always were better at lying than I was."

Her grin widens, like I've just given her the best compliment. And I guess I have. I've never talked with a Malryx, but this isn't any Malryx. This is Marsa. The girl who I thrust toward evil to save us all. The world may now be brighter, a world we can live and survive in. But she came out darker. Darker, perhaps, but someone worth fighting.

A noise sounds to the side.

"Lover boy is here," Marsa says.

Strange. As much as I thought I needed him here to face this, I forgot to keep track of how soon he would be here to help. I may love him, but there's much I can do on my own.

"We'll meet again soon," I say.

"Sooner than you think," she says.

My heart lightens and races, not with fear but with the impending excitement. I go against my instinct and turn away from her.

Jorrin is walking toward me. "She's getting away."

I turn back and watch her retreating form.

A smile escapes me. "I know."

The End

More by Janeal Falor

Mine to Tarnish (Mine #.5)

Katherine's place is the same as any woman's—on the shelf next to the dresses and bolts of cloth. When she's sold to a warlock, life grows even bleaker. Her new owner is as old and rancid as he is cruel, driving her to do the unthinkable: run.

Nothing prepared her for being on her own. And she's definitely unprepared for the warlocks hunting her down. But she must stay one step ahead because if caught, the best she can hope for is death.

You Are Mine (Mine #1)

Serena knows a few simple things. She will always be owned by a warlock. She will never have freedom. She will always do what her warlock wishes, regardless of how inane, frivolous, or cruel it is. And if she doesn't follow the rules, she will be tarnished. Spelled to be bald, inked, and barren for the rest of her life—worth less than the shadow she casts.

Then her ownership is won by a barbarian from another country. With the uncertainty that comes from belonging to a new warlock, Serena questions if being tarnished is really worse than being owned by a barbarian, and tempts fate by breaking the rules. When he looks the other way instead of punishing her, she discovers a new world. The more she ventures into the forbidden, the more she learns of love and a freedom just out of reach. Serena longs for both. But in a society where women are only ever property, hoping for more could be deadly.

Mine to Spell (Mine #2)

Cynthia has always hidden from her father's hexes behind her older sister. When her family gains independence unheard of for women, she's relieved that her days of harsh punishments are over. But as her seventeenth birthday approaches--the typical age to be sold to a new master--death threats endanger her sisters. She now faces two options: run or meet society's expectations.

For once, Cynthia isn't going to let her older sister shield her from the problem. She's going to prove to herself, her sisters, and society that her family isn't a threat to their traditions. She willingly chooses to be purchased by a new master. A bold step that takes her somewhere she never thought she would go and to a man she might possibly fall in love with. With his help, she may just find a way to save her sisters while discovering how to stand up for herself. If she lives long enough.

Acknowledgments

Thank you to my awesome sister, Karen C. Eddington, who is supportive with my writing. And to Michelle Pasket for always being willing to help not only look over my manuscripts, but help make them better. Huge thanks to Loralie Hall for reading and always being there to bounce thoughts, ideas, and keep me company at conventions. You're the best!

Thank you to Kristen Halligen for reading and pointing out my sneaky grammar slip ups. Sarah Canning, big thanks for pointing stuff out and becoming a partner at helping other authors. You so Rock.

My editors super rock! Thank you to Yesenia Vargas for helping clean up my work. And Sotia, paranoid editors make the best editors! Thank you for working so hard to make this book better!

The biggest thanks goes to my family for continually supporting my with the joy I find in writing. To Rebecca for making me laugh and helping brighten my life enough to write. My kids for being so awesome at helping give me ideas and being so fun to play with. A most gigantic, loving thanks to my husband, Erik. You are my life.

About the Author

Amazon best selling author Janeal Falor lives in Utah with her husband and three children. In her non-writing time she teaches her kids to make silly faces, cooks whatever strikes her fancy, and attempts to cultivate a garden even when half the things she plants die. When it's time for a break she can be found taking a scenic drive with her family or drinking hot chocolate.